In memory of all the Roma, Sinti, Jenisch, Dom and other largely forgotten victims of genocides.

Robert Dawson

LEAVES IN A HOLOCAUST WIND

AUSTIN MACAULEY PUBLISHERS™

LONDON • CAMBRIDGE • NEW YORK • SHARJAH

A CIP catalogue record for this title is available from the British Library.

ISBN 978-1-78693-717-9 (Paperback)
ISBN 978-1-78693-718-6 (E-Book)
www.austinmacauley.com

First Published (2017)
Austin Macauley Publishers Ltd™
25 Canada Square
Canary Wharf
London
E14 5LQ

Which seat should I have? Oh that, OK, opposite you, sir, and Zuzzi next to me. Thank you, lieutenant. Yes thanks, sir, we know who you are, and that we can take a break whenever we want, but we just want justice. We're just a bit worried about the court and what it will be like there when we're in the box giving evidence, with us being Gypsy people – still, that isn't yet is it, and you say it might not even have to happen.

Anyway, we decided that we'd each tell bits and keep swapping over from one to the other. Zuzzi wants me to go first. I'm going to start eight years ago in autumn 1938 and Zuzzi in 1941.

The war between Germany and England hadn't yet started – we were in our teens then – and you could still travel around quite easily. But I must start at the beginning.

DEMETER'S TESTIMONY (FOXY)

One

My name's Demeter Fox, but my nickname is Foxy – all Romany people have nicknames though I don't hugely mind what you call me as long as it's not insulting.

I'm nervous because really this is such a big thing to make a statement about what we witnessed for the Allied War Crimes Commission and if I think about some things too deeply, I get upset.

I suppose I've got to begin a long way back so you'll understand it all. I'm Romany – a Gypsy – well, you know that. What you don't know is the connection. You see, way back in about 1904, about 80 of my people went over the English Channel to England with their wagons and horses. They wanted to do metal work and make and mend pans and kettles and what not, but people were very afraid and suspicious of us, even though there were Romany people in England already. Everywhere my family went, all through England and into Scotland, police went with them and that made things worse because people thought we must be dangerous. Eventually, all the family gave up and caught a ship from Scotland to Brazil and later made their way back to Slovakia, which is where they came from in the first place.

Actually, that's not totally true because not all of them went to Brazil – three stayed behind. Those three all married English Romany men – one called Boswell, one called Ryles and one, who was my Grandma, who married a Romany called Fox.

Anyway, when I was about eight, my mum and dad both died in a wagon fire – I don't want to talk about it and I don't even know much about it, as I was too young. My Granny, who was about 60 then, brought me up but then decided it'd be better for me and her to go back to her relatives in Slovakia. My English Romany relatives were fine, but they didn't follow the old Romany ways quite as much as her family, she used to say. I don't think that's true, I realise now that there was something else going on which I didn't know about but partly because it was late spring 1939 and the terrible war was soon to begin, though I now think Granny knew much more from her second sight. We packed up a few clothes into a hessian sack each (we had no suitcases) – I didn't have many things and nor really did she – and set off on the long journey to Slovakia. My father's family gave her a lot of gold coins and she had some herself so were able to buy tickets on the boat to

France and then on trains – one was called the Orient Express – and from Budapest we went into Czechoslovakia. On some of the trains there were German soldiers who bullied everyone and Granny seemed quite afraid of them. They pointed at us and laughed and I kept hearing the word "Zigeuner" I thought maybe the clothes we were wearing marked us out.

We reached a place called Poprad, as Granny's family were usually somewhere round there. Poprad's a lovely town and it's a holiday resort and it has lots of old buildings – still, that's nothing to do with this. She had distant relatives in some old houses in the town, ramshackle ones no one else wanted. They made us very welcome and after a night's rest and some good food, one of them went with us into forests situated near some mountains to guide us to Granny's near relatives. We walked for a good hour then he gave a loud whistle. Romany people all have whistles, which are signals for each other and soon after, one of the scruffiest people I'd ever seen appeared. He knew Granny Vee Fox straight away and gave her the biggest hug you could imagine.

"Nephew Vanta," she cried, almost dancing with delight. His delight was even more certain than hers. He did three cartwheels across the forest floor, gave a huge leap and did a perfect handstand, actually balancing on his head.

"Woof woof," he barked.

Two

"You must be Prefikany," he said, grabbing me in such a hug-hold I thought I would never breathe again. The word meant nothing to me – "Foxy"! He gave me a low bow, pulling his hat off and sweeping the hat through the air to rest it on his thigh as if he was an actor. I must have looked blank: "It's Slovak, means Foxy," he explained. "Or if you prefer it in the Romany, Lallo-jukkel."

That I did know, though I was never called it in England. He spoke to me in our own English Romany and it was only later that I thought how odd this was and wondered how he had come to learn to speak it so well and yet also speak the Eastern European version of the Slovak Gypsies. He took Granny's big carrying sack from her and my much smaller one and hoisted them onto his back, where they hung, from behind, like huge swellings, making him look three times his normal width and now our guide from the town left us with our grateful thanks and returned home.

"Come," he said, "this way. My wagon's only a mile or so away." As we walked, he and Gran talked together and sometimes to me, whilst I studied my distant cousin. I would estimate he was well over six feet tall, but looked much more because he was as thin as an English hop-field pole. In fact, when I got to know him better, I often wondered how such a human walking skeleton could manage, because he had so little flesh on him and none of it which wasn't essential.

My clothes were shabby to say the least. British Gypsies in those days rarely had more than two sets and though I was wearing my best tograms, I was very conscious of the patches in my trousers, which Gran had tried to make look like a part of the design, and the small tear in my shirt, yet next to him, I looked like a city gentleman just up from London.

He had long wavy hair which hung over the back of his head and at the sides like a black kitchen mop, almost to his shoulders. He wore an ancient blue jacket and red trousers, like those worn at strict attention by soldiers on ceremonial guard at airports when a VIP arrives. He even had gold braid – tatty I grant you – sewn onto both the trousers and the jacket, underneath which an open-necked white shirt almost hid his brown buckled belt. His boots? None! The first thing I had noticed when he did his handstand, was his bare feet, sunburnt brown on top and dark brown leather-like underneath.

He saw me looking at his feet. 'Your feet get used to the forest floor and the paths and the roads," he said. "Mind if someone GAVE me his boots I'd wear them. Pity, yours are a bit small," and winked at Granny Vee.

"Don't your feet ever get cut?" I asked in wonder, imagining all the hard and sharp surfaces they might encounter.

"Oh, hardly ever," he said. "Except those pine needles are a curse when one gets between your toes and stabs you. But in the name of the Good Lord, am I not a Gypsy and has not the gracious Lord God given us all the free medicines we could ever need in these same woods and the fields nearby to heal such things?"

Granny Vee had already taught me a lot of plant medicine but it was Uncle Vanta who was to teach me even more in the brief months to come and also how to live off the woods.

Uncle Vanta's wagon would have been shameful to many an English or Welsh Romany person. It was simply a very basic cart and over it some hoops and over them rough canvas, much patched. In England, our very basic wagon was an Open Lot and they were palaces beside this, for they were longer and a little wider and heavier, though still light for a wagon, and some even had a stove, like the more sophisticated wagons of other types. The only British wagon to compare with Uncle Vanta's was what were called 'Accommodation' wagons, basically a two or small four-wheeled cart with a tent structure on top. They tended to be more for people to keep their belongings dry when they travelled.

"Come," he said, "Make yourselves at home and rest before we go on."

"But where are the others?" I asked.

"Five miles yet," he said.

"But why are you not with them, Uncle?" I asked, fearing he must have some sort of disease or social problem. He wasn't my uncle, but we call older people uncle or aunt as a term of respect.

"Because, m'boy, I'm the advanced guard and the lookout and the yapping dog and the mad one in the family." I must have looked shocked.

"He doesn't really mean mad, Foxy," Grandma explained. "What he means is that someone lives away from the main camp in the direction from which visitors are most likely to come so that visitors can be intercepted and checked if they are safe or not and so warn everyone. But someone living separately from everyone else looks very suspicious as if we have to have good need for a look-out, hence he pretends he is a bit simple, that he has learning problems and behaves in a strange way."

Now the barking and the cartwheel and the handstand began to make sense.

"Even other relatives?" thinking of our guide of earlier on.

"Sometimes, even relatives unless they are of our immediate band, because there are bad Gypsies as well as good," said Vanta. "So, I make others think that we Gypsies are an odd lot and people to be kept way from. Not that we're doing anything wrong, but we're different and that makes people suspicious."

A dog under the rickety wagon watched me closely as if it wasn't sure I was to be trusted. Vanta groped under his home and pulled out a bottle and some rough metal tumblers from a cupboard underneath. "The king himself is using our best tumblers today," he grinned. "So, we have to make do with second best. Fiftieth best really."

Uncorking the bottle, he poured a generous lot into each. "What is it?" I asked.

"Just drink," he said, so I did.

Three

The dark liquid ran down my throat like molten lava. I felt the heat rush to my face.

Vanta laughed uproariously. "Sip it boy, sip it!" he said. "This is strong stuff – my own-make gin generously flavoured with sloe," and he laughed again. "It is too strong for young foxes – it'll turn the foxy streaks in your hair white!"

He was referring to a patch of gingerish fox-coloured hair at each side of my head, surrounded by the black, which was how I got my nickname, not simply my surname. From then on, I sipped tiny bits. In fact, I didn't finish my tumbler until Granny and Vanta had finished their third.

There was still a little left in the bottom of mine when Vanta took the beaker back. "You have done well," he said. "It is an acquired taste. Probably I should have put good woodland stream water into yours. Anyway, let us be off."

He tossed the bags over his shoulder onto their bulging back situation and strode off, Granny at his side and me scampering after. All the time, the dog watched me, its nose down on its paws but showing no sign of wanting to come with us.

'Can I call the dog?" I asked. Maybe he'd like a walk."

"He wouldn't," said Vanta. 'He's old and rheumaticky and anyway, he's the reserve guard to look after things in my camp."

He said it so sternly I took it as a sign he wished to speak to Granny without me taking part. I listened to what they had to say as we stepped along a wide track skirted by a range of trees and grassy knolls, bushes and patches of flowers.

"Have you seen the Germans?" Granny asked.

"Oh yes, but they do not bother us. The ordinary people are very frightened because there are stories of them rounding up Jews and there are many children of El who live round here. I suppose they want them to work for them, I don't know. Anyway, we see nothing of them here in the woods. Why should they bother us?"

"I am not convinced. In fact, I am worried," replied Gran.

"Oh?"

"These are not like ordinary soldiers who have a quarrel with more soldiers from somewhere else. They've taken Austria, the Ruhr, Sudetenland and Czechoslovakia simply taking what they wanted and done it with ease. They haven't yet finished and now there will be war. The trains were full of Germans, all laughing and joking, putting their feet on the seats, swearing at the train staff, drinking, singing bawdy songs. They think it is all over, they think that everything is theirs, that they can do whatever they like. That means everyone who is not Nazi is in danger."

"N'aw, I cannot think that." Vanta did a quick cartwheel. "We're Gypsies, my dear aunt; we matter to no one. We have no argument with anyone – in fact, we might even do well by playing our instruments for them and the women and girls dancing for them. As they are the victors, they will have plenty of money – other peoples' I grant you, but money."

Granny shook her head vigorously. "If we play for them, it will be the devil's tune and if we dance for them it will be the dance of death and ghosts."

"I had forgotten what an old pessimist you are," he laughed. "You didn't want us to go to England in the first place, they say. But what did you get from that? A husband, a son and a grandson."

"But a dead husband, a dead son, a dead daughter in law, and I can smell death here, too, terrible death."

I could not stop myself. "What do you mean Granny Vee?" I asked, fearing her reply.

"Aaah, now you're frightening the boy," said Vanta. "There is no need for all this gloom. God has given us the forest and the sun and the rain and the moon and the diamond stars. Why should we talk of death?"

"Because it comes."

"What do you mean Granny?"

"I cannot tell you now, boy, but you must listen to me, and listen to Vanta because I have decided you will live with him now and not in the main camp. I want him to teach you all he knows, the fiddle of course, but also the cures for people and animals because you will need them and even more about the foods of the forest."

"But, Granny, I want to live with you and with the others."

"Oh, you will still see plenty of me and them, but as you know, I have the second sight and I see you have a job to do, though not yet and I'm not even sure you will succeed."

I plucked up courage. "Are you always right, Granny, in your second sight?"

"Usually, not always, but I'm confident this time. First, Vanta must get you ready for the quest which you have ahead of you."

Quest? I didn't know what she was on about.

"Quest?" I asked. "What do you mean?"

I never got an answer for at that moment, Vanta gave a shrill two-note whistle and in the distance, I heard a two-note reply.

Four

Moments later, two Gypsies emerged from the bushes at the side of the track. Both were young people, but older than me and they were introduced.

Lazzy was a boy of about sixteen and wearing a fine suit of rags – torn jacket, torn shirt, torn and over-short trousers, a floppy hat and he had bare feet. His black locks hung down to each side of his face, brushing his shoulders. He gave me a low bow and I began to wonder if this was a normal Gypsy custom here, because it never happened in England.

With him stood a most beautiful young woman, his sister Petal. Like Lazzy, her feet were bare though only just visible under a long flowing red dress with what looked like blue dahlias imprinted in the design all over. She wore a loose orange-yellow blouse buttoned tight to the neck, as is the style of all respectable Gypsy women, and her beautiful shiny black hair was adorned with a strange covering which looked like a cross between an old-fashioned headscarf and a red cap. I learned later that they were twins, though you would never have guessed it. Petal gave me a modest hug.

I found their Romany language hard to understand and they knew not a word of English nor I Slovakian but this made me realize how unusual Vanta was, since his Romany speech was much more like that of an English Gypsy, but he was too young to have been an adult in the 1904 party in England. As we walked, my distant cousins tried to tell me their versions of Romany language for different things – trees and their names, animals, flowers, and lots more. After about thirty minutes, I was beginning to remember some of them when Lazzy signalled us to stop. He gave a two-note double whistle like Vanta's earlier, but then immediately repeated it twice more.

In response, I heard a cuckoo cry, then a host of young children burst from the woods like elves and clustered round us, shouting and tugging at our clothes. Vanta shouted at them, "These are our family, not our enemies. Leave them, leave them," but they were doing nothing harmful, and were obviously just very excited to see us.

Two small girls gripped my hands, one at each side, and jabbering unintelligibly tugged me off the track and down a broad pine needle path. A small boy had hold of Granny's hand, despite her scowl, whilst several clustered round Vanta, Petal and Lazzy like excited puppies.

"They are the cavalry!" Vanta called to me, moving more slowly than my little side engines allowed me. "Dangers come to Gypsy camps, people wanting to harm us. It is their job to charge out at visitors, to ask them questions and to put people off who have not come for the right reasons so they trouble us no further – but we are not trouble, children, not us!"

I was tugged into a clearing in the forest. Of course, I was used to Gypsy ways but this was so different from my English relatives. The six wagons were all very shabby and two were of the accommodation type I mentioned earlier. Three more were very shabby and battered looking and only one would have stood a second glance from my English Gypsy relatives back home.

No dogs barked – in fact I only saw two scruffy things which looked like they might be relatives of Uncle Vanta's cur. I could see only one horse, tethered at the edge of the clearing, but there obviously had to be more somewhere. In the centre of the clearing stood one large cooking fire with several pots and kettles clustered round it. This in fact was only one of three really familiar things to me, though with the number of people there were here, there would have been several fires had we been in such a camp in England. The second was the large number of hens which seemed to run hither and thither everywhere, or which perched on wagon steps and roofs. The third, not quite so common in England, three nanny goats tethered at the edge of the clearing, their bags obviously bursting with milk.

But the enormous difference was the way the people dressed. I was used to Granny, her apparel marking her out from the rest of the women in England and yet not so dissimilar as to be strange.

Granny Vee almost always dressed the same so that when she changed her clothes, it was simply into a clean version of what she had taken off. Unlike the other women in the camp, and more like her English kin, she sported a headscarf tied tight round the chin. Her dress was long, almost touching the floor and always dark green. On her feet was a pair of black lace up boots such as a labourer might wear. Her blouse was simply a piece of hessian sack-cloth but over this she sported a long dark green cloak with two hoods, one for her head and the other for putting in anything useful which she found on her travels, or any bits of food she had managed to beg. Under her green dress were several thick petticoats, the outer of which concealed at the front, two massive and useful pockets in which she held an array of items she just might find useful as the day wore on – I never discovered the full range, but over the next couple of years I witnessed small scissors, string, red ribbon, a rabbit snare, a twist of salt, two bandages, a little jar of some sort of ointment for an undisclosed purpose, a liquorice root, several lucky charms and various others I cannot now recall. Romany women, of course, are very strict about modesty, but it never troubled Granny to lift the front of her green dress a few inches to get at the pockets as her legs remained discreetly covered under all the petticoats.

People here dressed differently.

Five

Of course, it didn't matter that they wore different tograms from what I was used to. It's just that they were so different it made them into a sort of uniform, so you could have recognized them on any street in any town, down any lane, as Romany people. I was glad about that because these were my people, my relatives and they were proud to be different and that made me proud too.

All the women wore dresses similar to the girl Petal, long ones which almost trailed the floor. They were usually red but sometimes blue and always patterned with contrasting flowers. Their blouses were of linen, commonly white and bleached in the sun, but sometimes mid-blue, rarely anything else, and on top a sort of wrap-round waistcoat of rough material, I think hessian. All were bare footed.

The men's wear was very different from Uncle Vanta's. All wore long white linen shirts which overhung their trousers by many centimetres, and the trousers themselves, though they varied a little in colour with shabby blue, patched brown and scuffed red being the favourites, were fastened over the shirts as well with broad leather belts. Over all these they sported either scruffy wool jackets, or occasionally wool coats. Some were bare footed but more wore ancient boots, I supposed to protect their feet because of all the time they spent gleaning in the forest or working with hot metal and hammers. Their hats were usually uniform, similar to a fedora in style and almost always grey or occasionally brown. Several of the men had bags over their shoulders on diagonal straps – tool bags, I learned later.

The white shirts of both the men and the women often had colourful embroidery sewn on, in the form of patterns or flowers, usually red.

Children's wear was more varied in colours, the girls all wearing long red, orange, blue or green dresses from shoulder to ankle with thick wool shawls over their heads and round their backs, all of different colours from their dresses. Boys invariably had smaller versions of the menswear.

Another thing all had in common was long black curly hair which hung down over their ears and shoulders,

Now all the camp came out to greet us, with excited cries and people running to Granny Vee and all wanting to hug her at once. The exception was a tall and hefty man, dressed as the other men except his belt was broader and sported a silver buckle whilst instead of a fedora he wore a Cossack hat.

"Good afternoon, boy," he said. "I am Sherro Rom." If it was meant to impress me, it did, because I knew that all Gypsies in Eastern Europe had two very important figures in their communities, one being the Sherro Rom, which just means Chief Gypsy. You might think his was an inherited job through family or because his father or grandfather had been Sherro Rom, but that's not so. The Sherro Rom is elected by all the people in the extended family. They sit down round the fire and decide who they want and they take a vote on it, though usually it doesn't need any vote. What they look for is the luckiest and cleverest Gypsy man and ideally – but not necessarily – a strong one. His job is to make all the important decisions on behalf of the family and say when or where we are going, how we will prepare for the winter, when marriages will take place, whether to spend money on new tools or homes. He also has to negotiate with outsiders, especially when they threaten danger.

I gave a small bow as one should to a respected person, something I had thus already learned from Petal and Lazzy.

"So, you are Granny's red dog, eh?"

He patted me on the head. His Romany was more guttural than mine but he spoke slowly, realizing I would find it difficult.

'Uncle,' I replied respectfully, with another bow.

"Come," he said. "Sit with me at the fire. The Poori Dy has told me about you. She says you have a task to perform for us all."

I must have looked puzzled. "Later, later," he said.

We squatted cross-legged at the fire, in the traditional Romany way, and moments later food and drink was brought to us – a bowl of traditional stew from a massive iron pot on the fire with brown bread to dip followed by a huge slice of wild raspberry pie with goat's cream. In fact, almost everyone came and sat round the huge fire, perhaps seventy people including the children, Vanta and Granny sitting near me and we all tucked in with gusto.

People shouted questions to me but unless they spoke slowly – which they hardly ever did – I found it difficult to understand and Granny had to translate for me. We sat there long into the evening, conversation dying off, until the sound of insects and birds disappeared and the only sound was the crackling of the fire interspersed with snatches of song. Then Sherro Rom pointed to a small rough tent which stood near the best of the caravans. "You can sleep in there tonight," he said. "And we can talk more in the morning."

It was a well-appointed ridge tent and though small had several blankets and a pile of dried grass and plants as a mattress and I was soon blanket-wrapped and snuggled into the forest-plant mattress and fast asleep.

Six

I need to explain more about my Romany family.

I say they looked different, looked like Gypsies, but looks are not the person. Granny's relatives – my relatives really, too – were just lovely people. There wasn't an ounce of badness in any of them – they were brim full of love in everything they did. They were also brim full of mischief and humour, because all Gypsies enjoy laughter – Granny used to say that if we didn't laugh we'd cry because of all the terrible things done to Gypsy people. Mostly they laugh at themselves or each other but they also laugh at more-than-my-job's-worth officials who try to make their lives difficult and most of all they enjoy tricking the pompous and pretending to be stupid or deliberately misunderstanding.

Yet it is the music which I think most people know Gypsies for, some of the finest in the world, and did you know, lieutenant, sir, that many of the most famous composers heard our music and wrote it down? They changed it a bit and those pieces are some of the most loved in the world.

Anyway, the next morning I thought the Sherro Rom would talk to me and ask me questions, but he didn't. His wife gave me a huge breakfast of fried eggs and black bread. As I wiped the grease off my plate with a bit of bread, Granny Vee came and sat by me at the fire, which someone had revived from the night before.

"Demeter, I told you that I want you to go and stay with your Uncle Vanta," she said and by using my real name thereby told me she was very serious because it was the name she normally reserved for when I was in trouble or something serious was going on. I waited for her to explain. "The world is changing, my boy, and not for the better for Gypsy people. Terrible things are coming, things which I can see, but which you could not even understand, for they are so huge, so terrible that they are almost unbelievable. I've told you before, you have a job to do."

She had said it often, but I had always thought of it as being a job like working for a living and perhaps doing quite well. She must have read my thoughts.

"This is a special job. Wicked people are coming, people who will devour us – they are wolves, but worse than animal wolves. They will sweep through Europe and they will tear away the flesh of all Gypsy people forever if they can, and not just Gypsies – anyone they do not like."

I was finding it more difficult, not less, to understand. "But who are these people? Can't we hide?"

She shook her head. "They will find us wherever we are. There is nowhere to go – wolves on the hunt smell people out, they creep up on them in the night and attack when they are not expected. You must not be here. That is why you must stay with Vanta, so you are safe."

"If they are coming here, when? And why do we not all move on?"

"Because I don't know when, and even if we did move, they would find us still. You are my hope to tell others and to make sure the wolves are caged."

"But, Granny, how could they even find us here? We are deep in the forest and we have the watchdog people and plenty of time to disappear into the undergrowth if we need."

She took my hand in hers and held it gently. "When the breeze blows, the leaves on the ground are disturbed. When the wind gets up, the leaves are tossed into the air and they have no choice what happens to them. They may float for a while, but eventually they will fall to earth, who knows where. And if they land in some garden or the grounds of a rich man, they are swept up and burned. If they don't, they die and decay anyway."

"But, Granny, if something is going to happen I want to be here to help look after you and to get to know all my family better. Maybe the wolves will not come."

"They will and so you are to go with Vanta. You will see plenty of us still, every day if you wish. Vanta will be your teacher and you will learn a great deal from him. Listen to his wisdom and to his knowledge so later you can use it for the good of everyone. And do not be fooled by his foolishness – he has forgotten more wisdom and knowledge than most people will ever know."

So that is how I came to be with my wonderful Uncle Vanta, the camp watchdog, the camp sentry and the camp doctor and the finest naturalist imaginable.

Seven

The next few weeks and months were some of the most wonderful of my life. My only fear was that somehow, something would take such great happiness from me. Uncle Vanta had a rough tepee style tent made of long sticks cut from the wood and pushed into the ground to make a pyramid shape. Over the outside were stretched several pieces of overlapping course linen and bits of serge material. The cone centre was open to the sky because immediately under it we would sometimes have a fire, either for warmth or bits of cooking though mostly cooking was done on another fire outside. Sometimes, when the rain was bad and we had no fire, Uncle Vanta threw a piece of canvas over the cone to keep the water out. Our mattresses were dried grasses perfumed with Meadow Sweet. His primitive wagon was a chemist's shop and storeroom as also was the area under it (next to the dog) but we never slept in it because it was jammed full of his medical things.

We would sit throughout the evening and into the night whilst he told me, oh so many things; folk stories full of heroes and villains, fairies and giants; stories about my own family's history and the things that had happened to us, good and bad, in the past. I learned of our alliances with other extended families and why it was largely good for Gypsies to trust each other, but with a few notable exceptions. He taught me Slovak, enough to hold a reasonable conversation with someone anyway.

Above all, I learned more of Granny Vee and why she was considered so important – she was the new Puri Dy after the death of the last one. That came as a surprise, but not a huge one because of the massive welcome she got from everyone at our first arrival. With the Sherro Rom, she was therefore our leader in all things. Above all, she imparted wisdom and knowledge, healing and folk medicine, knowledge of animals and birds and their ways and how to respect them and not least her second sight which she used to guide the Sherro Rom when it was necessary.

Every day, Uncle Vanta took me deep into the woods to show me plants which were useful for healing. I learned to make ointments, poultices, anaesthetics, even a type of cotton wool dressing from plants. I learned how to find birds' nests and from them take, if needs must, one (but only one) egg, without disturbing the other eggs so the adult bird did not realize. He taught me to respect all animals and birds and never to harm any unless it was essential that I had to.

He even banned harming insects. I hated wasps having been stung several times in England, but he just left them alone and they seemed never to trouble him. Bees he adored, and had me watch them closely through an old magnifying glass so I could see them in the flowers, feeding with their long tongues or collecting pollen or nectar for their young. He taught me to never breathe on them as in bee culture it is considered very rude. I actually learned to hold my breath for long spells as a result.

Sometimes, when we were on a woodland path, we would come face to face with a snake. One which terrified me was a sort of blue-grey colour, but Uncle said it was totally harmless; another, copper red, was likewise. The only one of any danger was the adder. When we met one, Uncle would take off his hat and give the snake a great bow. 'Excuse us, my brother,' he would say. 'May we come past you? And within a few moments the snake would slither into the long grass and allow us through.

We often saw deer – red, fallow and roe – and they trusted Uncle so much that he could feed them by hand. He was very against anyone killing them to eat but sometimes he would find antlers which had fallen off and these he prized both as tools and as simple medical instruments.

There were many foxes and it was common to notice them watching us. Uncle said there were wolves and bears in the woods, but I never saw any though I once saw a lynx. One day, we were picking toadstools for tea – Uncle knew exactly which were safe – when there was a rustle in the undergrowth and a large boar stood before us, two baby piglets by its side.

"Ah," said Uncle. "Climb a tree quickly." And I needed no second invitation. He did not, however, follow but just stood stock still. The boar approached him, smelt him and then walked on with its young.

He signalled me to come back down. "People have been so cruel for so long to the boars that they think all humans are enemies to be destroyed. They know me and know I am harmless, but they do not yet know you and would have attacked you. Treat them with great respect. I always did and they eventually got used to me and though they were always wary of me, they never attacked."

The other great lesson I learned from him was which plants and fruits and nuts were safe to eat and when the Great Mourning of our people happened, that knowledge was so important to help us to survive as wild creatures ourselves in the wood. There are so many things you can safely eat and in season lots of variety – angelica, wild roots, nettles, dandelion, acorn bread as well as lots of nuts and wild fruits to name but a few.

We used to dry herbs and plants, hanging them from the low branches of trees and bushes, but some plants, like nettle tops which he stored for his animals, we simply spread on the grass and let dry in the sun. He had two goats and dozens of chickens. Strangely, with foxes in the woods, he never ever lost a single hen to my knowledge, but he said that was because hens were not as stupid as people thought and they roosted high in the branches of trees. I suppose they could have flown off had they wished, but then, why should they when they were with Vanta? They supplied us with masses of eggs and occasionally, when a bird was old and Vanta decided it was suffering, he'd wring its neck and put it into a slow cooking stew pot. But we ate little meat otherwise, though at the main camp meat was almost always on the menu and I did not then mind it.

The old brown dog with its long floppy ears – which Vanta had given the name Dog to – never seemed to move from its place under a cart. Several times I sat by it and stroked it and talked to it, but though it would lift its head and cast mournful eyes on me, it never responded. I did not think it was much of a life for a dog until Vanta explained it was well over 20 years old and that Dog had earned a long rest. Vanta's donkey was not much better – it spent almost all its time grazing and totally ignoring people, especially me. I don't know what happened to it.

Eight

Though we spent so much of our time at Uncle Vanta's camp, on most days we also went to the main one because Uncle Vanta frequently had work to do there, people or animals with injuries or illnesses.

I loved those times, especially when we stayed long into the evening and partook of traditional Romany zumin, which is a sort of stew or thick soup. After we had eaten, tales would be told round the fire and we would all crowd in and warm ourselves at the prospect of ghosts or ghouls creeping up behind us. Then the fiddles would come out and we would sing and dance. Round about midnight, we would make our way the five miles back to Vanta's camp, because he did not like to be away too long, so we rarely slept over in the main camp, but with our way lighted by the moon and the stars, I got to know the paths to Vanta's and other tracks so well that I hardly needed light.

On those evenings, my very favourite thing was the traditional Gypsy dancing. There was one small girl called Roopy whose dancing was astonishing. I suppose she was perhaps ten or eleven years old, younger than me anyway when I first met her and sometimes I dreamed that one day, when she and I both grew up, we would marry. I would have liked that. We were kindred spirits, she and I, and though I now love Zuzzi to my very soul, that love came from the need to protect each other from evil whilst Roopy's was the love of joy and freedom.

Oh, those dances, if only you could have seen them. When she went with the men musicians into town, with me accompanying Uncle Vanta, she would twirl and twist with her plaits spinning round her so she looked like a Catherine wheel and the people would throw coins to her which her little sister picked up into an old's bird's nest – well, so it looked, though it was actually a home-made rough basket, because there were no spare hats.

But beside our fire in the evening, her dancing was altogether different, for it was proper Gypsy dancing just for us and we understood its meaning even when done by a ten-year-old. Sometimes she was a flower in the breeze, her plaits out, her wild hair flowing round her face almost like a gauze mask, and you could smell the sun and the pollen and imagine the seeds blowing from plants; another dance, she was a young filly, tied by a rope and desperate to escape, her head tugging and receding, her legs pushing the earth to try to snap the rope.

Another was as a young deer in the forest, first grazing ever watchful, twisting and turning, ever looking for enemies and at the sight of one, leaping and bounding. Or she was just a little Gypsy girl, cavorting, jumping and twirling for the sheer joy of being alive. One she called 'leaves in the wind, and she really did make herself look like an armful of leaves, twisting and turning and blowing and landing.

To tease me, now and then she would do a special dance for me which she called prefikany – foxy. That dance was different from all the others or so I thought because it was my special one. Without moving from her place standing in front, she would appear to be walking stealthily sometimes and with brisk steps at others or with a trot, whilst her head always sought for smells of food or danger, moving round almost back to front, up and down, to each side. Then she would give a sudden leap in the air, a fox after a butterfly and twist round and round as a fox chasing its own tail.

Oh, how that little girl could dance, oh how I miss her and weep for little Roopy. Her full nickname meant 'silver feet' but Roopy said it all. Her little sister's full name, the girl who collected the money, meant 'pretty flower' but it was always abbreviated to Raykani or, more usually, Rake.

I was so happy; it felt like heaven. Then the grey wolves came and they devoured Silverfeet and Pretty

Flower and Petal and Lazzy and all my friends and all my relatives and even Granny who I'd thought was indestructible and – and me, in a sense. I'm sorry; I can't help the tears. Can we pause a moment?

Nine

Sorry about that. Anyway, on our visits into town, we often saw Germans about, but they never troubled us. I used to go with Vanta who'd been teaching me the fiddle and used to play a little with the men, but of course I was amateur compared with them. I also used to play little tunes for Uncle Vanta to do his 'mad man' act and his cartwheels and his dog woofs. The German soldiers had never seen his odd performance before and they found it very funny and threw coins, but, of course, the big earner was Roopy who everyone loved. Meanwhile the women would be trying to tell fortunes – Germans or anyone.

But our normal customers, who bought the metalwork or had pans or kettles repaired, were now reluctant to even answer the door because of fear of the soldiers though no one ever said why. When the men went into an inn to 'slake their mighty thirsts they got an inkling why – apparently, they had been rounding up the Jews and taking them away though no one seemed to know where or why. Mainly they took men, but also some of the women, though they didn't seem bothered about the children then from what we could hear and everyone presumed they were taking them somewhere to work for the Reich, because it was well known that the Nazis hated the Jews for some reason.

We never realized that they hated us, too, and if you ask me why they did, I honestly don't know to this day. Why did they kill us? Is it because we were free and had no places to stop in and that was not allowed anymore? The birds are free, but they have their trees or their nests to stop in. Or did they see us some sort of savage, primitive people who obey no laws but those of nature – untrue though that perception be. Why do all you non-Gypsy people not talk to us, find out how we are just humans like you. When you do not talk to someone, you talk *about* them and misinterpret them.

On the day the wolves came, Uncle Vanta had remained in his camp and sent me to the main one with some special tonic or medicine as there was a woman having a difficult pregnancy. Uncle had hundreds of medicines and ointments and poultices and stored them in a variety of jars and bottles in boxes under the old wagon (next to the dog). I'd been helping him make them up, so I had a good knowledge of what was what anyway.

It was a bottle of something to give the woman strength, he said, and I walked happily along the track to the main camp. I'd only been there a few moments when I thought I heard three shots in the distance and a single bark. So did some of the others, but it didn't worry us as gamekeepers shot in the woods and sometimes the local count came in to do some shooting as well.

Suddenly, we heard vehicles. Even that wasn't unusual because occasionally someone would go along the main track for logs or the like, but this time there were several vehicles and coming not just along the track, but leaving the track and coming to us. We all stood and watched. They had come from the usual direction, Uncle Vanta's. Yet there had been no whistle and they had passed by the advance watchers, too, before they even had chance to give us a late signal or for the children to mob them. Bewildered, those children followed the vehicles into the main camp.

There was an officer's open car and three or four motorcycle combinations with machine guns mounted on the front of the combination part and five lorries. They stopped at the edge of our clearing and an officer came out of the open top army car, which also had a gun mounted on its bonnet.

You could have sliced bread with the immaculate creases in his grey green trousers. His grey-green blouse had white piping round the shoulder pads and on the collar a double lightning flash whilst on the other collar were three pips. A white eagle was sewn on his left arm and over the blouse were leather straps attached to a belt from which hung a pistol and ammunition pouches. The belt buckle was real silver and depicted a swastika and an eagle. One thing made him look very sinister. His peaked cap had an emblem on the front – a silver human skull. It was much later that I found that these monsters were the infamous SS.

He had about thirty soldiers with him, most carrying rifles or a few light machine guns, and they jumped down from the backs of the lorries. They did not look nice, but they made no threatening gestures towards us, just stood together quietly talking to each other and exchanging cigarettes. The soldiers' uniforms were similar except that they had what I think are called forage caps on their heads and several wore camouflage smocks over their tunics.

Our women must have guessed there was danger because they made no attempt to approach them to tell fortunes. The officer shouted an order in German and a private soldier trotted forward. "I am the Herr Officer's translator," he said in good Slovak.

The breeze held its breath.

Ten

The Sherro Rom and Granny Vee, in her capacity as Puri Dy, went up to him. Sherro Rom gave a low respectful bow.

"I have both bad news and very good news for you," said the officer. "The bad is that the Herr Reichmarshall Goering has decided that this forest and the fields and the mountains are to be a large hunting estate for him and for his friends and for devoted workers for the Reich. At this very spot is to be built a fine hunting lodge, so, obviously, that means you will no longer be able to keep your wagons here."

"Sir, where can we go?" asked Sherro Rom. "It is difficult, sir, we have women and children to look after and feed. The forest is our mother."

"But that, my little Gypsy, is my good news: Herr Reichmarshall Goering has spoken to the Herr

Reichmarshall Himmler who is in charge of resettlement of people and he has decided that you will be given part of this forest for your very own – it will be your own property."

"Ours, sir? Ours to keep? But won't the Herr Count who owns it...?"

"The forest is now owned by the Third Reich, not some privileged master. Your Count can be 'counted out of the picture'," and he chuckled at his own joke.

"That is most generous, sir, thank you, thank you very much on behalf of us all. May we ask, sir, where this piece of the forest is where we can stay?"

"Not far, about eight miles away at the north end, a beautiful spot, overlooking the lake and with a view across the fields to the forests and mountains, which is beyond all description. You will see I am right."

We knew the lake, a glorious piece of countryside indeed which was teeming with the finest fish of which I admit we partook regularly. There were many rabbits in the fields and in the mountains, lots of mountain hare. We would even be able to graze the horses on the edges of the lake.

I saw Granny's face – it looked like thunder. She ambled over to me – "Garav!" she warned me. I didn't know why she was telling me to hide, I just couldn't understand, but the fact that she said it in Romany made me realize she did not want the soldiers to understand and that it was urgent. I did not move.

"Garav!" she snarled, adding that I must on no account come out of my hiding until the soldiers had gone, no matter what.

I slunk carefully away, taking Granny's glare with me, and slipped into the undergrowth, watching yet longing to be there with the rest and puzzling over her order which seemed ridiculous.

"We wish to stay here" said Granny. "We are doing no harm here. Give us this land."

"Madam, you are most ungrateful," the officer replied through the interpreter. "We cannot let you stay here because of the danger. Hunts will be going back and forth through this clearing and the chances are some of you would get shot. No, you must move. Your new location will be permanent – you can stay there forever and no one will move you."

Some of the camp mumbled and did not like what Granny had said.

"See, your own people see the sense of what I have said," the officer continued. "Your own land with no one to move you away. Yours for generations to come. We need to get you there today, but of course nothing is ready. We will take all your men and youths in our lorries to the place where you can work to get the place prepared and meanwhile the ladies can pack your belongings."

"Yes, sir, what tools shall we need?" asked Sherro Rom.

"None, we shall supply all your needs. The main thing is to dig latrines – no more sneaking behind trees eh?" and he gave Sherro Rom several friendly slaps on his cheeks. "There will be German ladies coming into the forest in future and they hardly wish to see you people relieving yourselves in public, eh?" he chuckled. From my hiding place in deep undergrowth, I couldn't see Granny's face, but she was standing rigidly like a hare frozen in a spotlight.

"Yes, sir," said Sherro Rom.

"Good," said the officer. "I think we can get you into two lorries and the ladies will follow in the others later with their essentials. You can come back for the wagons this evening or another day. Tonight, you can sleep under the stars – it will be a dry night."

"Yes, sir." Sherro Rom indicated for the men and boys to clamber up into the lorries and once in, several soldiers with guns joined them. Two motorcycle combinations, one at the front followed by two lorries and then the other at the back.

I suspected nothing and I even almost walked out to join them.

Eleven

Grandma stood stock still.

The sound of the vehicles disappeared towards the north and the women set to work with a will, packing up belongings and putting them into wagons or making bundles to take immediately. I heard snatches of excited conversation amongst the women, wondering what this place would be like. The Germans, through their interpreter, told the women to pile their belongings which were due to go immediately into one place and then had the women throw their bundles into the back of one of the lorries. The Germans would not let them put the cooking pots and kettles into their lorry, explaining that when one of the other lorries came back they would go into that. Neither I nor the women understood why that had to be the case, what difference it could make. Still Granny did not move a muscle.

Gently, courteously, they helped the women up in to the lorries along with the children. They smiled and held the children almost lovingly, passing them up to their mothers with such care.

"Oh, wait a minute," said the officer through the interpreter. "We must have a photograph of you good people. Corporal!"

"Sir!"

"You lead the convoy with the ladies and take them to their new home. The sergeant and I and three or four others will follow shortly in the last lorry after we have taken a photo."

I noticed Granny was fiddling for something in the storage petticoat under her capacious dress. A knife, I wondered? Whatever it was, she held it aloft and called to the leading soldier. "You" she said. "You will be as this is." I saw she was holding the dried root of Gentian, a bitter herb used as a fungal treatment, above her head. She held it high in the air and crumbled it between her fingers, letting the bits fall to the ground. "The dust of the earth to be trampled on and despised with bitterness for the fungi you are."

A flash of anger crossed the officer's face, but he said nothing and called to a group of young women who had been standing back ready to climb on the lorries after the more senior women had got on. "Ladies, let us have a photo, you beautiful ladies and a few German soldiers to show people how good we are to you Gypsies. We noticed a nice grassy bit just back there with the sun shining through a clearing. Perfect for a photo. This way."

The other lorries started their engines to set off after the men folk. One remained behind and the officer beckoned the young women to follow him. From my hiding place, I watched as the women, including Petal, walked off with Lazzy as the representative of the men, who had remained behind to be the women's chaperone, as is our custom.

All this I saw from my hiding place and suspected nothing.

Grandma still stood stock still, as if she was frozen, even her expression never changing so far as I could tell. Two soldiers got onto the motorcycle combination and led them all down a woodland track. When the soldiers had disappeared with the young women, I thought it must be OK to come out and I started to emerge from my hiding place.

"Kekka, Kekka!" Granny shouted. Hearing her order not to come out, I went back into the undergrowth. "The wolves are upon us," she called. "Witness, witness. The Great Devouring has begun." I pondered what she meant. The Romany word she used translated as 'devouring but it could also mean 'destruction or 'burial. It was a word which had an insulting meaning, too, like savage rape and not a word to be used lightly.

"Granda," I whispered. 'What do you mean?'

The interpreter said, "Help the old lady up into the transport." He indicated Granny, and two soldiers shouldered their rifles and took her, gently, by the arms and led her to the back of the last lorry. She was protesting but not struggling. One picked her up and slid her over the lorry tailboard where I saw others of our family help her in. 'See you later, Granny,' I thought. The lorries set off.

I could hear the soldiers laughing from the direction they had taken. I thought, they're having a good time with their picture. The laughter was suddenly overtaken by screaming and wailing and crying and it was obvious that a terrible calamity had fallen on them. I thought of Granny's use of the words 'wolves' and 'devouring'. Were the soldiers eating the women? That was a ridiculous idea. They were so polite, so gentle – and I was convinced they could not be cannibals.

The soldiers were shouting now, overshadowing their raucous laughter. The laughter faded and with its fading the moans of the women got louder and more distressed as their screams abated to short agonized bursts of weeping.

I skirted through the thick undergrowth about ten metres from the forest track and something warned me not to go along the woodland track itself so I could not run, but I staggered and pushed through brambles and thorn bushes, hardly noticing the tears at my flesh, to get to them as quickly as I could. I felt for my knife and realized I had left it at Uncle Vanta's.

A new sound: the stuttering, sibilating rasp of gunfire followed by about three individually spaced shots. I knew what had happened. I did not believe it possible nor understood why, but I knew. I broke out of the fox trail and onto the woodland track to get there the faster and had to leap from it and hide quickly as the sound of the returning motorbike came towards me. I peered from a patch of bracken: wisps of smoke drifted from the end of the barrel of the machine gun mounted in front of the soldier in the bike sidecar. They looked happy. Oh, I longed for a weapon myself, but knew I was powerless. Oh God, oh God, oh God.

Twelve

The awful ice of truth began to freeze on me. In my mind, I saw a vision of a massive storm at the break of a new day, a storm to blow terrible wind with snow, cold and hail, to lash and tear, to rip asunder the very heavens and destroy everything in its path.

When I was sure the soldiers had gone past and no more were coming, I broke free again onto the track and ran as fast as I could. I knew the little clearing and I knew what I would find.

Seven young women and girls, one young man, a baby. Lazzy lay alone at the edge of the little sunlit clearing, his arms thrown apart as if in shock, blood on his neck and chest. Maybe he had tried to run for help, or maybe he was the first to die, I don't know.

The others, their clothing awry, blood stained, Kresta with her baby son Fyno, nearby Maria, Rose, Salomi, Jezzy, all defiled.

Separate from the others, my two loveliest lady friends – Roopi Silverfeet and Petal, the girl who had special dances for me and the girl who I had met on my first day.

I knelt beside Roopi and pulled her dress back down over her knees for her modesty's sake. Her mouth was wide open and there were tears in the corners of her eyes which were open as if she was staring at something wonderful in the sky. For sure, it could not have been a leering soldier's face, but perhaps an angel or a great prophet who came to her at the moment of death. I gently closed her eyes. Petal's were already shut, but, again, I rearranged her clothing and then that of the others.

The grief came. I roared and wailed, threw myself onto the ground and beat it with my fists as if it was to blame. Repeatedly I kissed Roopi's cooling forehead, screaming, weeping and wailing constantly, tears streaming down my face until my ducts had no more tears to produce. If Vanta's knife had been in my belt, I would have plunged it there and then into my heart so that I, too, could follow my lovely kin to whichever of the seven after-lives was theirs, or if somehow they did not have one, at least I would welcome the darkness.

When I heard the motorbike returning, I only just had time to leap away into the undergrowth. I watched the men climb off the motorbike, take their rifles ready to use them, and start searching the little clearing. I could not understand their actual words, but guessed they had heard my loud grieving and had come back to kill a witness who had somehow survived the murders, or so they thought. I even considered coming out from my hiding place to let them kill me, too, but then Granny Vee's various words and warnings came back to me: "You have a job to do ... the quest which you have ahead of you ... on no account come out of hiding until the soldiers have gone, no matter what... the wolves are upon us ... witness, witness ... the Great Sadness has begun."

It felt like a steel barrier had come in front of me to stop me leaving the undergrowth. Now the soldiers pushed at the bodies to see if anyone was alive, then searched for bloodstains on the ground leading away; they shouted and hit bushes with their rifles to drive out anyone who might be hiding injured. I stayed. My hatred for them was only surpassed by the knowledge that foxes can hide well and will not be seen when they do not want it.

After a few moments, they kick-started the combination and bounced off back down the track towards the main camp area. When all was silent, I set off in the opposite direction to find Vanta, ever on the alert for the smell of cordite or soldiers' cigarettes or the sound of voices or machines. His camp was much further away from the murder clearing than the main camp – over four miles certainly – but I think I covered that distance in little more than twenty minutes, charging along the familiar pathway. Heedless of the danger, I burst into his clearing.

Thirteen

My eyes searched for Vanta but I could not see him. Maybe, I thought, he had heard the shooting of the women and had run back towards the main camp and I was just about to follow when I saw where Dog lay, on his side in the middle of the clearing. A huge patch of blood coated his side and had puddled on the ground. It was not hard to work out what had happened – he had been shot. The only question was if he had been trying to protect Vanta and if so, had Vanta escaped?

I searched the camp hoping to find Uncle hidden. I checked the undergrowth. I called his name softly. There was no sign. Hope deserted me and I started to search the camp for any traces of blood in case he had been hit but had managed to get away even so.

"Vanta, Uncle Vanta!"

I was frightened all the time that the soldiers may come back and had to keep my ear alert not only to the possibility of Uncle moaning or moving wounded somewhere but also the return of the enemy.

I fanned out from the centre of the camp in a spiral until I reached the undergrowth at the edges, but there was no sign of blood and the undergrowth itself had not been disturbed like you would have expected from someone having tried to run off through it.

'Vanta, Uncle Vanta,' I whispered again.

The only place he could have gone was down either the path which led to it or the one in the opposite direction. I had already been along the path from the direction of the main camp and had noticed nothing there, but I went back to it and searched more diligently for blood or tracks. Nothing. I headed off down the path which led away and eventually to the nearby village and to the town but, again, could find no trace as far away as the boundary of the village.

It gave me hope. If I could not find him, maybe he had escaped and was still alive somewhere in the forest!

It was a hard task to decide what to do now. The awful grief I felt at the loss of so many people I loved so dearly gripped me and jumbled into my thoughts so that I felt confused, angry, uncertain. Since I had not found Vanta, though, I still had some hope, so I tried to pull myself together to make a good decision.

At first, I wandered disconsolately through the forest and back to the original camping ground. The sight that met me there tore through me. Granted there were no bodies, but the desolation was too awful to view; abandoned caravans, hens wandering about aimlessly, dogs welcoming me because they knew my scent, but looking to me to do something to help them. There were no horses and I realise now that the Germans had commandeered them. I felt like I had been given a huge burden to carry. I considered staying there in the camp and living there – a stupid thought because I realised that the Germans could well come back to see if any survivors had done just what I was proposing to do, so to remain there would be very foolish and very dangerous. Instead, I searched about and found tools that I decided would help me, such as an axe and a knife, matches, and clothing suitable for me then headed off into the deeper part of the wood to find somewhere suitable to hide. Fortunately, it was not raining. After some aimless wandering about, largely moving north, I came out upon quite a broad track which I had to cross. There was no sign of any people and I guessed it was simply a track used by woodcutters or possibly hunters when they were taking their quarry away on a small handcart or whatever. It was not a track that a normal vehicle would be able to go on, but I guessed that four-wheel-drive ones would have no difficulty.

Fourteen

Being near that track made me feel fairly confident of my safety and I wandered into the wood at the far side. Perhaps 100 m from the track I came upon very thick undergrowth which I worked out would be a good place to create some sort of shelter to hide in and protect me from bad weather. Getting through the undergrowth meant crawling through a small hole, possibly one which had been used by animals such as foxes or perhaps even boars.

At the far side of the hole, it opened out into a little oval shaped clearing about 30 meters long and 20 meters wide carpeted with tufty grass and wild plants. When I looked at the hole I had just come through, I saw that it was underneath blackthorn and other prickly bushes which increased my confidence still further. In fact, most of the bushes round that clearing were also ones with thorns. There were a couple of other small holes under them which I thought might give me an escape tunnel if ever I needed one. I could not remember exactly where the camping ground we had used was in relation to this place and simultaneously I realised that some canvas from the old camp would be very useful indeed.

With the axe, I cut some branches and wove twigs round them, covering them with leafy branches to form a small rough shelter. I ate some of the food I had brought and settled down to sleep for a very disturbed night full of sadness and nightmares. The noises in the forest did not worry me in the slightest because they were exactly the same sort of noises that I was used to hearing every night at the camping ground and especially where Vanta and I had lived – it was the sound of the mourning in my own soul which kept waking me.

Next morning, I was up early, tucked the knife and axe in my belt, crawled out through their little entrance tunnel, crossed the woodcutters' track and entered the wood at the far side. I looked for traces of my journey from the previous day, such as snapped small twigs or foot marks in the undergrowth, but I had left little evidence, so this time I also marked my passage with vurmi, information signs used by Gypsies, consisting of bits of leaves apparently accidentally caught on twigs so that I would be able to find my way back more easily another time.

It was a lot further to the camping ground than I had expected and it took me a whole two hours to get there, though it is not impossible that some of the time

I went round in spirals rather than using more direct routes because I simply could not see well enough through the trees to help me find the best way. I saw the edge of the camping ground beyond the trees ahead before I got to it and made a cautious approach, but there was no sign of anyone there, let alone the Germans, and no sign that anybody had been there since the day before. I went round the caravans finding more items to use back at my new camp and especially finding pieces of canvas to make a better shelter. I stuffed as much as I could into three sacks and put them over my shoulder. The hens gave a squawking as I left as if pleading with me to stay and feed them, but all the dogs had disappeared except one old bitch which started following me. I did not mind that because I knew it would be lonely otherwise and it might even give me a little forewarning if my hiding place was discovered. After a while, though, the bitch gave up and turned back. In one of the sacks I had put in what food I could find, a few more men's clothes which looked pretty new and cooking utensils whilst in another was the canvas from tents and a few bits and pieces I thought would be useful. Following my own vurmi back to the track and then to my new abode was very simple and I began work straight away making a tent using the branches I had cut before and the canvas. I can't claim that it was luxurious or even a very good design of tent but for my first effort at making a tent I didn't think it at all bad.

The following day I made my way back to the camp and from there returned to Vantas's place. Here,

I loaded myself with several of Vanta's medicines and herbs which I thought might come in useful. There was also a small handcart which I very much wanted to take because I would be able to carry more things, but though I could have got it back to the main camp I could not see how I could trundle it through thick undergrowth to get back to my new home, so I left it.

Fifteen

In the days which followed, I made several more visits both to the main camp and to uncle Vanta's, collecting more items. The old dog began to follow me back to my place every time, but I didn't encourage it and after about half a kilometre it always gave up. At one time, there had also been three nanny goats tied up at the edge of the main camp, but by now there was no sign and I wasn't sure if they had been taken by the Germans for their milk or meat or whether they had simply escaped and were now wandering somewhere in the forest. Once again, I would have loved to have had a goat as company and milk, but it was impractical and dangerous.

The fate of my family was always on my mind because although I knew what had happened to some of the young women and girls and suspected I knew the fate of Uncle Vanta, I had no idea what had happened to the rest of the people, even though I was sure they were all murdered.

So, one morning when I awoke early, I headed north towards the lake expecting to find some clue there. There is quite a wide track through the forest which goes in that direction and was the one taken by the German lorries days before. I was very cautious about using it in case there were still any Germans about, but the only sounds I heard were the normal ones of the forest. The track emerged from the wood at the top of a hill which overlooked the lake. It was a track which all Gypsy people had used over many years and one of the first things I saw was our vurmi of a bit of cloth tied to a twig. It gave me no hope because I knew it was an old one, there to tell other Gypsies that we were in those woods. But almost alongside it I could see, at the edge of the trees on the very top of the bank above the lake, a large long mound of brown earth. It took no imagination to realise why it was there or who it contained and I did not have either the heart or the courage to dig down to confirm what I was sure was there. Instead, I looked around down towards the lake, but could see no one. I wanted to leave a vurmi of my own on the mound so I made my way cautiously down the slope to the edge of the lake and round to where the stream went into it. The lake has steep sides and the water quickly gets deep but there is a shoreline at the top. At the stream, I selected two white and two dark stones because that is the way some of my people show that Gypsies are present. White depicts females and dark stones males and large and small show adults and children. I took the stones to the mound and carefully pushed them just into the top so that anyone passing near the old vurmi would spot them and realize that there was a connection, that there were both males and females but the oddness of just two stones of each would make them question what I was about, though no one could have guessed the horror of what that connection was.

I'm sorry about my tears, I'm OK now.

Some groups of families always used the same vurmi so it was possible to identify which family had passed by from the little detail of the vurmi, like a scuff on the bark of a tree or wavy lines left on a stone. Mine would give no such clues.

By the time about three weeks had passed since the massacre, I had begun to be quite proud of my little home which I had constructed and improved. It was of an ideal size for one person so that I could lie across the back of it to sleep in a nice bed of dry grass and leaves, but at the front I put an old box for a seat and made a fireplace outside the entrance and a porch to keep the rain off. Of course, I knew that I could not possibly have a fire in daylight because smoke might have been seen and betrayed me. In any case, I had little need for a fire except for warmth because most of my food was what I gathered raw from the forest. My only other food was bits that I had managed to recover from the main camping ground, most of it tins, and an occasional wrap of tea. Every day when the weather was reasonable I used to go out to what I called gleaning to find food.

I saw, too, that I was beginning to make a track from the edge of the cart tracks to the hole where I went into my own little terrain. So, I put a pile of small dead branches and twigs to one side of the path and each time I came back from somewhere I scattered some so as to disguise the path. Similarly, because I entered the forest at the far side to go to the main camp, there were obvious traces of human passages so once again I put twigs and branches over my entry point to hide it. That was much easier because there was no reason why anyone would go into the forest there if they did not know that there was a track.

Already the caravans at our old the camp were beginning to look abandoned and unkempt and grass was beginning to grow over the debris of the camp. I had pretty well taken anything of use from there by now, but there were still quite a few medicines at Uncle Vanta's place which I had left because I did not then discern I would need them.

Whenever I cut a branch from a tree to use for some purpose, I was always very careful to rub dirt onto the newly visible stem of the tree so that no one could tell that it had been cut recently.

One day, I went on a gleaning trip towards the mass grave and the lake. Just as I emerged from the track, I saw a figure skirting the edge of the lake, being already two thirds of the way round and having passed the stream with the special stones. I slunk back into the bushes to see what the figure was going to do. I could not tell if it was a man or a woman, but he or she was wearing a dark jacket and what look like a scruffy short brown tunic over a pair of grey trousers. As I watched, the figure gained the bottom of the hill and glanced up towards the track. I sank further into the undergrowth and watched as the figure climbed the hill and reached the beginning of the track. I still could not tell whether it was man or woman, but he or she studied the old vurmi and then looked at the vurmi made from the stones and for a moment I wondered if it could possibly be another Gypsy, but I knew that to be impossible because my extended family were the only ones in this area and I knew, too, that they were no longer here. Then the person began to whisper-sing an old Romany tune, *Where are you?* and my hope leapt, but I was still not sure if it could be a trap - one set by the Germans to find me. That probably sounds paranoid now, but if you'd been living as I had, hidden from murderers, then I think you'd be paranoid, too. I moved silently as only a Fox, round the person, grabbed them round their waist and held my knife to their throat. "Who are you? Speak or die."

ZUZZI'S
TESTIMONY

One

I'll start at the beginning, too. Everything changed for Foxy, and everything changed for me, and my family as well, because at one moment we were happy and doing our best to earn honest livings and the next ... the next. I'm crying already, sorry.

We were living in France. I suppose you'd say we were French Gypsies or Romanies, but you see Romanies have no country, no land to call theirs, we just moved about and stayed mostly at the edge of the forests and went into towns and villages to earn money. The women told fortunes, the men mended metal pans and kettles or anything they could, or made new ones and sometimes made brushes if there was no metalwork to do.

We were a mixed group of intermarried Gypsy tribes, and we saw ourselves as both Manouche and Romanichal. Manouche is our name for ourselves and the Manouche are some of the most famous musicians in the world because it was we who invented jazz, not as you might think the black people in America, though they adapted our jazz to their own purposes to make a new kind of jazz which we also love. Really the guitar is our favourite instrument.

Two of our men were horse whisperers. Maybe you haven't heard of such things. Farmers would ask them to call to look at a sick horse and pay them when the horse recovered – they mainly did horses or sometimes donkeys and other animals. The true horse people in our family were Kekkanav (my grandfather) and my uncle Lon. Horses are valuable animals which were needed all the time to work on the farms so they paid well, which was why Grandfather Kekkanav was easily the richest person in our large extended family. He even had buttons made out of gold on his jacket – not his every day jacket, of course, just the one of the three which he wore on special occasions. Both men never went anywhere without their 'horse bags' since you could never be sure when a farmer might want instant help. Mind, it wasn't only horses – they were often needed to help cure goats or cows or anything for that matter. I suppose you would say that they were vets, but they had no actual qualifications and couldn't even read or write, but they understood animals, they could read them like a book, oh yes. In the bags were various herbal remedies, alcohol and herbs to kill germs and a couple of very sharp knives and thick cotton thread and needles to sew wounds. I used to try to always go with them when they went to farms and smallholdings and watch how they treated the animals and I learned a lot from just watching.

Kekkanav was our leader. Foxy will tell you how leaders are made amongst Romany people, but the point is it's done through having great respect for and trust in someone, and we all then agree – even the kids – that the person will be the best. That person has to make important decisions and do his best to keep us safe.

We had heard sounds of war such as distant gunfire, but it hardly bothered us. They said that in the north, the French army had been heavily defeated by the Germans and that the British army had to escape in boats across the channel back to England. But we didn't really care much – oh what foolishness. We hadn't been fighting anybody and we had no intention to, though some of the young men from other Romany families had been called up into the French army. If anything, the war probably helped us at that time as some of the farmers had lost their workers into the army and so they sometimes wanted us to do little jobs for them, like fencing or helping with the hay and again we were paid but always a fair price.

Of our band of about fifty, we only had three or four who would have been eligible for the army, but their call-up must have been missed because Kekkanav kept us all away from non-Romanies except for times of actual earning, the only exception to that being in an evening when sometimes the local mayor would decide to hold a dance and he'd invite some of us to go to the village hall and play the music. I and my cousin played fiddles – everyone agreed I was a very good player – Bas had a mandolin and Sasty a guitar, whilst some of the women would dance like crackling flames from the fire and all would cheer. We were not paid, but instead we had permission late in the evening to go amongst the people with Kekkanav's hat and collect coins for us all to share and by the time the audience had tasted a few wines, they were often more than generous.

Then it all changed.

Two

When we went into the villages, we sometimes saw German soldiers, but more often they were in the towns. They did not bother us and we hardly bothered them. They had no interest in our metalwork, of course, but the women tried to tell their fortunes and usually they let them and took it in good part and paid well. I and some of the other musicians would play for them in the street – they used to ask for traditional Nazi songs which we gradually learned and for which they tipped handsomely.

We did not understand why they had come into France, especially our part of the land, but they really did not seem too bad at first. Someone said they had been sent here by someone called Hitler, who was an evil man, but we were told by villagers never to say anything bad about Hitler to the soldiers or they would be angry and throw us in prison, so of course we didn't.

Maybe our big mistake was with the horse, I don't know, because it brought us to their bad attention.

We were on the outskirts of a little village and the women had gone ahead of us to do fortune telling and I was about to follow. A few of the old people had remained in camp to prepare our evening meals on the fires, and I was playing the fiddle to advertise us.

We could hear shouting going on in what we took to be German. Approaching the outskirts of the village we saw a German soldier on horseback, and several on foot. The man on horseback was shouting and (I presume) swearing at his horse and lashing with his whip across its back. Suddenly, the horse gave a low moan and collapsed and the rider was lucky to be able to leap off at the last moment so his leg didn't get trapped underneath.

Our horse whisperers, Kekkanav and Lon rushed forward and I stopped playing instantly. Fortunately, the officer spoke French.

"Sir, sir," said Lon. "We are experts with horses. May we help?"

"Huh," said the officer, kicking the horse. I saw now something ludicrous about him and it was all I could do not to giggle. His nose was a most peculiar shape. It came down straight as a ramrod until it reached the bulbous bit where it was distinctly round, with a crack in the middle, so it looked like a miniature bottom on his face. I've never lost his picture from my memory and I only have to think 'bum nose' and I see him. "The creature's had it." He pulled a revolver from his holster and pointed it at the horse's head.

Kekkanav pleaded. "Sir, please let us see if we can help. It is a fine animal and not old." The chestnut brown coat which should have been shining was dull and matted and neglected looking.

Bum Nose thought for a moment. "Very well, but when it dies you can have the pleasure of burying it. Understand? If I come back here and find it still by the roadside, Gypsy scum, I will find you both and you can go into the ground with it. Go on, let's see what you do."

"Thank you, sir." Both men threw themselves on the ground. Grandfather Kekkanav began whispering in the horse's ear whilst Lon tried to soothe it with stroking. "Pass my horse bag," he ordered. The horse was making soft whimpering sounds. Uncle spoke to it in Romany so the soldiers did not understand. "I know old friend, I know. They have treated you very badly, but we are here now and we want to make you well." He looked at Lon who nodded and held a hand out for his own bag.

"Sh, sh," he said.

"You're an idiot," said Bum Nose. "Fetch another horse," he shouted. One was brought from somewhere at the back of the column and the saddle transferred by a soldier from the sick animal to the new one. "I've a good mind to shoot you now, Gyppo. Talking to it – the horse is not human, any more than you are."

Again, he drew the gun and levelled it, this time at Lon. "Get rid of the poxy beast," he ordered. "Or else."

"Yes, sir," replied Lon.

"Forward!" he ordered his men and they set off again, a troop of about fifty wearing combat uniforms, their rifles and bags slung over their backs. In the rear were a couple of carts which must have contained provisions and tents, I suppose.

As they disappeared down the road, Kekkanav said: "This poor animal has deliberately tried to kill itself – it wanted to die because of all the cruelty it has experienced and seen. We must convince it that we will love it and care for it."

I watched as Lon took salves from his horse bag and gently applied them on the cuts and bruises caused by the brutal whip on its back. Meanwhile, Kekkanav was feeling slowly up the underneath of its neck but I did not know why. When he had finished with the back wounds, Lon did the same, feeling against the animal's gut and stomach.

"Empty," he pronounced.

"As I feared," said Kekkanav.

He lay over the horse and whispered again in its ear. He was several moments and all the time the animal seemed to reply with little whimpers.

"Shh, shh," he whispered. He levered open the horse's mouth and peered in. "I will have to operate and I am going to need some things," he said, standing and shaking his legs and arms to get the circulation flowing in them again. "Zuzzi, I will need your help – it is a good lesson for you in nursing. Lon will be my assistant doctor."

Three

Granddad Kekkanav and Lon shouted for the things they needed and people began scurrying away to find them.

"Light a fire ... boil water ... find molasses ... find honey ... find wheat bran ... fetch a jug ... borrow a torch ..."

A score of willing helpers ran to houses to beg or borrow the items. Soon there was a crackling fire going on the opposite side of the road and on it a copper pan of freshly drawn stream water.

People began returning, some with more success than others. An old bulldog torch with barely any shine was grumpily rejected; Kekkanav showed pleasure when a large quantity of sugar beet molasses returned, but honey was not to be had anywhere. Probably it was well hidden from the Germans or they had found and taken it for themselves already.

"Send the children into the fields," Kekkanav called. "Have them pick all the flower heads they can find, especially big ones like dandelions – no stalks mind – and throw the heads in the copper pot to boil. And nettle tops – warn them about getting stung. Someone find wild garlic."

Kekkanav half lay on the horse whilst Lon stroked it. He whispered something in the horse's ear – it took several seconds. The horse gave a gentle whinny back.

I stroked the animal lovingly. The hair on his back was rougher than I'd expected but more downy towards his belly. "Ssshh," I said. "It'll be all right, trust us."

Kekkanav pulled the jaw down so the mouth was wide open and Lon put a wooden block from his bag into the front of its mouth to prevent it shutting its teeth on them.

"I can see it," Lon exclaimed, peering into the back of the mouth. "It's well lodged. If only we had a torch to see better – Zuzzi, angle the head more to the sun so we get all the light we can." I helped heave the head round, not that the horse protested or resisted but of course it did not know what we wanted it to do, so its head was dead weight.

"Tin snippers!" Kekkanav shouted. It was the sort of tool we used a lot because of our metalworking and a few seconds after, one was passed.

He took one look at the snippers and exploded. "This is a horse's mouth I'm dealing with here, not an old cooking pot. Smaller than these and make sure they are clean and very sharp. And hurry." It seemed to take a long time for a pair to be found and cleaned sufficiently and throughout I whispered to the animal and stroked its side. At one time, whilst we waited, I heard Lon say, "Patience, dear brother," and I thought he meant Grandfather Kekkanav until I saw he was actually whispering it in the animal's ear.

Carefully, gently, Kekkanav's hand with the snippers reached far into the horse's mouth. I couldn't see what was happening from my angle, but after what seemed an age, I heard a single click and a few seconds later a second one. Carefully, he took something from the mouth and held it up for us all to see – a piece of barbed wire.

Several of the family clapped until he shushed them. "I've not finished." He fished back into its mouth whilst I, at any rate, held my breath. The horse coughed violently. "It's no good," he said. "I can't get to it – my hand's too big."

"I'll have a go," said Uncle Lon, but Kekkanav stopped him.

"It needs a much smaller hand. Take over from Zuzzi, and you come here, Zuzzi." Lon took the head and I scrambled to my feet. "Wash your hands – scrub them," Kekkanav ordered, "And shake them pretty dry. Now," he continued when I knelt by him. "Look in the mouth right at the back. It's hard to see because we can't get much light there. There was a piece of barbed wire caught across the gullet, snagged at either end. I've cut the piece from the middle, but the two ends have to be got out, too. Now this is important. You cannot just tug them or you'll rip the poor beast's throat. Also, you cannot keep your hand there long because you could distress the animal, so keep your hand as flat as you can, feel very very gently with your fingers to the barbed wire where it is hooked, from the feel, push it gently out – I think it will be a push – and get out the first piece. You think you can do that?"

I really wasn't sure. "It's all right, it's all right," I whispered to the horse and put my hand in.

Four

It felt odd, in that I had to twist to the left of the block of wood holding the mouth and, sort of, slip forward over the tongue, past the long row of teeth and so to the back of the mouth and the gullet. I did it steadily, evenly, but now, keeping my hand as flat as a board of wood, I moved it very slowly and just touched the wire. The horse gave a little jump and a grunt so I knew I had hurt it even with that slight touch. I pushed my fingertips forward and touched the wire again. "Shh, shhh," I whispered. "It's OK." My fingertip touched flesh and a little bulge where the wire must have gone in. I closed my eyes, swallowed hard and pushed, gently but firmly, and as it moved, closed my fingers onto the wire. The horse gave a bigger jump but the wire was free and I extricated it and held it for Kekkanav to see.

"Good, good," he smiled, took it from me and threw it into the ditch. "A little rest now."

"It's OK," I said, "I'm OK to try and get the other bit."

"Not you, you fool – the horse needs a little rest. Meanwhile, I want you to put more stuff into the cooking mash. Then wash your hands and by then it'll be about recovered enough for us to continue. I want to get this block out of its mouth as soon as I can."

My Aunt Vurmi – her nickname – was stirring the pot. "What's in it so far?" Kekkanav shouted.

"Just the flower heads and the nettle tops and the oat bran and the chopped up wild garlic," Vurmi shouted back.

"Now add the molasses. Stir it well. Zuzzi, get the jug and fill it a good half full with liquid from the cooking pot – avoid bits as much as you can but a few won't matter. Then run to the stream and keep putting cold water in. Stick your elbow in and when it feels warm, but not hot enough to burn, it's ready. Then bring me the jug." I had a thousand questions I wanted to ask but I knew now wasn't the time so I scurried about my task, eventually returning with the jug of brown-grey liquid.

"Have you washed your hands?" I nodded and showed them to him. "Good, now go for the wire at the other side. It doesn't look as badly wedged so far as I can tell. It might be easier."

All three of us reassured the horse and Lon spoke to it gently in Romany, explaining that it had nothing to fear. There's a belief amongst Romany people that some horses can understand our language and certainly the horse seemed to because it remained calm as, gingerly, I stretched my hand to the right of the wedge, across the teeth and to the back.

My fingertips reached where the wire had been on the other side, yet, strangely, there was no wire there. I froze and Grandfather Kekkanav sensed it. "It is there," he assured me. "It must be further down the gullet than we thought. You'll have to be very careful now and when you find it, get it fast because the horse will be very frightened."

My hand moved back through the top of the throat, a hair's breadth at a time. The barbed wire strand was much further down than I had anticipated. In fact, when I touched it, the horse gave a huge retch and jerk as if it was trying to stand. We all shushed and soothed it and I had another go. This time, as soon as my finger touched the wire, I gripped it, pushed it free and pulled it from its mouth. The horse twitched in pain.

"Excellent!" said Lon. "Now move out of the way whilst we look."

Both men peered into the animal's mouth. "Good," said Kekkanav, "You've done a good job, Zuzzi. Only two tiny drops of blood. Now we need the jug. Empty the jug into the back of its throat, a bit at a time but so it has to swallow." Whilst Kekkanav and Lon held the horse's head, I slowly poured the liquid into the back of the throat, letting it swallow a bit at a time until the jug was empty.

"Excellent again!" said Kekkanav. "Now the wedge." Lon forced the mouth open a little more so the wedge would come out. I continued to shush it and try to reassure it. When the wedge was clear, the horse shook its head and slowly rose with a vigorous shake of its mane which caused his whole body to also shake. It was shaky, too, on its legs, but must have been heartened by all our family cheering like mad as it stood, staggering a little, shaking its head and mane a few times as if there was something of an unpleasant taste in its mouth. I stroked his neck and he nudged me with his nose.

Five

On Grandfather Kekkanav's instruction, I took the gelding back to our camp, walking it slowly and gently. Grandfather gave me very strict instructions for his feeding, for he was run down. He had to have plenty of molasses for a while and increasing amounts of good oats mixed with the bran and with flowers.

From being a weak, dispirited animal, he grew in strength and spirit. Daily I began taking him to good stretches of grassland for him to gorge himself and he obliged. He was such a fine chestnut animal, brown all over except for a white flash on his nose and with my treatment, his brown coat started to have a wonderful gloss to it. I brushed him regularly, spoke to him constantly, hugged him and, yes, even kissed him. He became quite skittish, dancing and prancing, playing with the dragonflies as if one moment they were fierce monsters and the next his best friends, leaping and turning, bucking, running sideways. He knew he made me laugh and my joy was unequalled. I loved that horse as a brother.

I gave him a name which in the Romany meant 'Leaf in the Wind" but I shortened the Romany to 'Bavalengro'.

Grandfather Kekkanav always told me I must never ride him but did not give a reason. One day, when the sun was warm and I felt too lazy to walk him back from a pasture to the camp, I decided I would ride. There was no saddle, of course, but we Romanies are used to riding bareback. I patted his neck, reassured him, held his mane and leaped on his back, yanking my skirts up so my bare legs could grip his sides. I clicked him, gave him a little dig with my heels and he set off at a gentle trot. That wasn't enough for me, so I gave him another dig with my heels and he broke into a canter and finally a gallop. It was one of the most exhilarating rides of my life, to have an animal under me and obeying me not because of fear or even duty but because of love, for that was what it was.

Gradually, I used the lead reins to slow him back to a canter, then a trot and a walk. I was tempted to try jumping but was less sure about my seat than his ability.

We trotted into camp and I felt like a hero, a warrior, returned from a conquest. "Look, Grandfather," I shouted.

He was in his wagon. He peered from the door, jumped down and strode towards me. I saw his face, puce with anger and glaring at me so that I realized I had committed some terrible sin.

"Get off that horse!" he shouted. "How dare you disobey me?"

"But, Grandfather ...," I began.

"I told you that you must not ride him," he shouted. "Why have you disobeyed me? That poor animal. You have betrayed me."

"But, Grandfather, he didn't mind at all. His wounds on his back are totally healed now."

"It isn't the wounds on his back, foolish girl, it is the wounds in his soul."

"But, Grandfather," I began, sliding off the horse and giving him a friendly thank you pat. "I've nursed him, he likes me – he's my horse now."

"You wicked girl!" he almost screamed so that my mother ran towards us wondering what was happening. He slapped me hard across the face – it was the first time I was ever slapped or hit by him or by any Gypsy and the last.

The force of the blow made me spin and stagger and had the horse not been there for me to grab hold of, I would have fallen over.

"Grandfather!" I screamed.

My mother snatched me in her arms. "She doesn't know, Father," she said. "She does not understand."

"Take her away then and tell her what a wicked thing she has done and how she has made me break my word," he said and turned his back on me and stomped back to his wagon steps and almost jumped inside in his rage.

My mother took me into our wagon. It was a small one compared with Grandfather's, really only a cart with hazel rods bent over and tied at the top and a sheet of canvas thrown over. We were not rich. We sat on some blankets and she pulled me towards her.

"You see," she said, as I sobbed. "That horse had been given a terrible time. It was the most unhappy creature upon God's earth, so much so that it had deliberately swallowed barbed wire to kill itself and it would have succeeded in time if we hadn't – if Grandfather Kekkanav and Lon - and you – hadn't operated, but at first the horse did not want an operation. Grandfather knew that if they tried to operate against the horse's will it would just struggle and make it impossible and even cause itself deliberate injury. It told Grandfather it just wanted to die because it was tired of being a beaten slave. So, Grandfather promised it that if it would let him save it, he would guarantee his freedom and that he could go and come or go away forever from all people and live wild if he chose, but that never again would he belong to anyone by grandfather's act. But you rode him and that meant he was no longer free but was

97

owned by someone – you. You broke Grandfather's promise to the horse."

"I didn't know!" I said. "Is it too late if I promise I will never to ride him again?"

'I don't know,' said my mother. 'But you must go and apologize to Grandfather and, of course, to Bavalengro."

So I did, and Grandfather forgave me my error and Bavalengro seemed to and nuzzled me to show he did.

Six

About a week after that, in the early mid spring of 1942, the Germans arrived in our camp along with several French gendarmes and officials of some sort who wore suits but no uniforms. We were stopped beside a large wood where we could get plenty of kindling for the fires and food from the clearings, the streams and our small animal traps.

I'd just gone down one of the paths into the wood seeking for Bavalengro, to make sure he was OK. He was free to roam at will by now, but I used to check now and then. I knew one day, Bavalengro would have gone because he was free, and I dreaded the day but knew it was something I would just have to accept. Bavalengro had followed me back to the camp in the hope of an apple and the officials and soldiers must have just arrived.

"Where is your king?" the officer asked in broken French."

Kekkanav walked up to him. "We have no king, sir, but perhaps I could help you."

"Are you in charge?"

"Not as such, sir, but I do have some influence. Is there a problem?"

"We are moving you," said the officer. "You will pack up all your belongings and hitch up your caravans. We are moving you to a town near here where we have created a special camp for vagrants."

"But we're not vagrants, sir, we're Manouche Romanies."

"It isn't a matter for philosophical discussion. You will obey my orders and do so quickly. We are busy people and have much else to do. In the morning, we shall send a police escort to take you to where you must go. And don't think about packing up and leaving the district meanwhile to avoid it because we will find you and bring you back and it will be the worse for you, I promise you. Do you understand?"

"Yes, sir, but I still don't understand why. We've done nothing wrong, sir, have we?"

"That is a matter of opinion. It is not just you, but all vagrants. You will find some more of your people already there when you arrive and more will follow."

There was obviously no room for discussion.

The next morning at about 8 a.m., two cars and a lorry load of police arrived, but there was no sign of the Germans.

We'd already packed except for the last moment cooking pots and fire irons. "You won't need those," said a police sergeant. "There will be no fires."

"But, sir, how will we cook?" Lon asked.

"Everything you need will be provided."

Several people started putting the big iron pots and fire props to hang on the backs of wagons.

"Not those!" the sergeant almost roared. He pointed at some on the back of Patteran's wagon and a constable went straight up to them, ripped them off and threw them on the ground.

"I don't understand," Kekkanav protested.

"It is not your place to understand but to obey orders," and he punched him, hard, in the face, knocking him over.

A sudden dread came over me. I backed away to the edge of the wood where I had seen Bavalengro sleeping that night because he had realised something was happening in the camp and we had been bringing in the wagon horses from their hobbled grazing which interested him. I considered leaping on his back and galloping away, but I feared grandfather's wrath but also that if I did, the gendarmes might shoot at me or punish my family – they did not look like nice people. I reached Bavalengro. Anyway, I was not about to disobey Kekkanav. The terrible dread squashed me, gripped my mind: I edged to Bavalengro, put my arm round his neck and pulled his head so I could speak in his ear. Tears flooded over me, but through them I was able to just about whisper, "Flee, Bavalengro my brother, flee! There is terrible danger. Flee for your life!"

He seemed to consider it for a moment, nudged me farewell with his nose, snorted, turned and set off at a canter, down the path and into a future of his own. I felt as if he had taken my heart with him.

"Right," said the police sergeant. "Harness up your horses and you will follow our car. The other car will tuck in after about the third or fourth wagon and the lorry will follow you – but any attempt at leaving the convoy or disobeying orders, and we have orders from the Germans to shoot."

It took several minutes, but then we were off, as the policeman had ordered. Mum managed to capture nearly all our hens and put them into the baskets we used to carry them when we were on the move, but some people's birds were uncooperative and had to be left behind.

When we Manouche move, the way we do it is small children ride in the wagons but adults and older children walk beside or behind their own wagon, the pulling horse being led by one of the adults. This is because if we all rode on the wagon, the horse would not be able to pull it or would tire quickly, especially on an uneven surface.

We were a sorry bunch: normally we sang and played our instruments when we moved, but not today. We were mostly blanketed in a deep melancholy and as the camping ground and the wood faded into the distance behind, and we passed from sandy tracks to narrow tarmacked roads, my fear and dread grew. I'm not saying I'm psychic, but I just knew something terrible was going to happen. I should say that I had a father and a mother and three younger brothers. The brothers seemed to see it as some kind of adventure and they were quite jolly, but I could see tears in my mother's eyes.

Seven

We travelled all morning and in the afternoon we saw ahead of us the beginning of a town. I was one of the few who could read, but as we passed the town sign, I said it aloud – "Drancy." At the time, it meant nothing to us. I think some of the older people had been there in the past, hawking and playing their instruments, but it wasn't somewhere I'd heard of. The police led us to a large field next to what I thought must have been one of the high walls of the town. What frightened me was that other than the wall – and there was barbed wire along the top of that wall – a large barbed wire fence surrounded the field, almost three meters high. There was a single double gate to allow entry and alert German soldiers, helmeted and carrying rifles, stood beside it.

The leading police car stopped at the entrance and the soldier beckoned us to pull our wagons onto the field. There were already half a dozen wagons there and though I didn't know the people, some of my family clearly did and were related distantly to them. My family waved, but the people already there gave desultory waves back. We stopped the wagons wherever we wished on the grass and were about to unhitch the horses when the police from the second car and the lorry which had taken up the rear, came rushing in, wielding truncheons.

"Not there, not there," they shouted. The existing wagons were parallel in a row and that was how they indicated we had to park, too, with our wagons parallel, leaving perhaps two metres space between them.

Normally, we keep a distance between our wagons and park by either leaving a big gap or so that doors are opposite each other so there is privacy but also companionship, but the police would not allow that. Kekkanav said nothing, I think he was too traumatized by the punch, but Lon tried to explain. Immediately, a policeman struck him with a truncheon.

"Just do as you're told, Gyppo," he said.

So we obeyed, and our wagons and the ones already there filled the whole of one side of the field. I think the men had intended to move the wagons during the night (so my mother said) when they thought the police would not be around, but before that could happen, as dusk fell, another batch of eight wagons appeared and were ushered in to park two meters behind us and again parallel.

The occupants looked tired and frightened. They were Lovari Gypsies and had been forced to travel almost non-stop for three days. The Lovari are horse experts, but you would never have guessed it. Their horses were old, not the fine animals they usually had when we saw them on our travels.

Up until this point we had not eaten, but one of the old women started a fire with what bit of kindling she could find, and was in the process of smashing up an old chair for fuel for the kettle when one of the Gypsies who had been there before us, rushed up.

"You are not allowed fires," she said. "Get it out quickly. If you make the Germans cross, they will shoot."

"But we have had no food, how can we cook?"

"You have to eat whatever you have. Raw if necessary. Quickly now."

We had a meagre supper of whatever we could find which we had brought with us and whilst we ate, the earlier arrivals watched us, it seemed longingly, I wondered why – later I learned that they were starving.

There were two taps with water on the field and six earth latrines which always stank and were supposed to be emptied by us every day into old oil drums on a cart which were taken away and replaced now and then with empty ones. By then, it was usually full and you can imagine the stench.

Late in the evening I strolled round the fenced field to get an idea of my bearings. I could not understand why they had put a fence round us to keep us in or what they thought we might do if we were not held here. And how long would we be here?

As I walked beside the fence at the far end of the field, I saw a German soldier, rifle on his soldier, patrolling on the other side, an Alsatian on a lead. He barely gave me a glance and neither did his dog, just ambled alongside the fence. I couldn't help wondering if we had somehow misunderstood and that they had put us here with guards not because they thought we were dangerous but because they wanted to protect us.

There were more answers next morning and I discovered the awful truth.

Eight

It was barely eight o'clock in the morning. Kekkanav and Lon and several of the men and youths had gone to the entrance gate to ask if they could be given work in order to get money for food.

Whilst they were still negotiating and finding out what they had to do to earn money, several German soldiers on horseback arrived. The guard let them in and through a megaphone, a junior officer spoke to us all:

"Now hear this. All your horses are to be requisitioned for the German army. They will be taken now."

Taking a Gypsy's horse is like stealing a Romany's heart, as I've already indicated about Bavalengro, but my one joy was that Bavalengro wasn't there and was still free, I hoped. We all loved the horses and a murmur of outrage went through the camp. It was then that I noticed the first arrivals standing near their wagons and realised that when we first moved onto the field, our horses were the only good ones there. Their fine animals had already been taken from them.

The soldiers began getting our horses and tying them with lead reins behind the ones they rode. I was so glad that I had told Bavalengro to flee so he, at least, would be free and not become a war horse. Kekkanav and Lon went up to the officer and though I could not hear what was said, I realised they were protesting. The officer just ignored them.

At that moment, I heard a commotion at the far end of the field. A German soldier had the reins of one of the old and skinny horses and its owner, a distant relative, was trying to pull the reins from his hands. Another German rode up and hit the Gypsy with a whip, but the Romany held on, then up rode the officer. He pulled a gun from his holster and pointed it at the man, obviously warning him to let go or be shot. He had no option and the horse was led away with all the others. Now we were even without our horses so could not have moved our wagons even if we had been permitted to.

No one protested after that – we knew it was both hopeless and dangerous and the men had got nowhere in their negotiation for work to get money for food. Rather, the guards said that to get any food we had to have ration cards. No one had ever told us about this so we hadn't got any. But the soldier said workers would be given a ration card.

We had another hungry night, but next morning, the junior officer arrived and through his loudspeaker he said there was work available for the Reich for anyone who volunteered. Every man did, including the first arrivals and the Lovari, and so did I and most of the young women, but they said we were unsuitable. They also rejected nearly all the men from the first arrivals, but it did not seem to come as a surprise to those people.

We tried to ration the little food we had, most of it going to the children, but about noon a small lorry pulled up outside the gate. The soldiers announced that, though we had no coupons, we would be allowed to buy food from the lorry. My mother grabbed what cash we had and ran for the gate hoping for some bargains. Actually, there was little variety – potatoes, stale bread, a few old vegetables, eggs, a bit of cheese, butter. We didn't need eggs as we still had our hens that'd come with us. The prices were colossal – someone would have to work for about one and a half days to get enough money for a scrawny chicken (not that we needed one as we still had our own), half a day for some stale bread and more than two whole weeks for some butter. Mum wanted bread, saying there was no purpose getting potatoes if we couldn't cook them (we had no ovens in the wagons and always had to cook outside, which we now knew was banned).

I learned later that the lorry came from the town every day loaded with food for sale, but it was always pricey and it got more so. The lorry man – I called him Thief – used to charge about three times the normal rate for anything. Apparently, the Germans sent a lot of the local food back to Germany for their people, making all the food they left more expensive. I also learned – I witnessed it – that the lorry driver had to pay the guards a bribe every day to be allowed to sell us the food.

Our men came back in the evening after a day's hard labour digging ditches and repairing and widening roads. They had been given ration cards and the next day would be allowed to use their first ration tickets on the way home if they had money with them. They had also had a meal at lunchtime of a hunk of bread, a bit of cheese and a glass of wine! I thought things were beginning to look up.

So I thought.

Nine

Next day, about 20 more wagons pulled on and the following day 12 more. The same happened as had occurred with us – the Germans came and requisitioned their horses and they were stuck on the field like the rest of us.

Within a few days we had learned just how awful our situation was. We were constantly puzzled as to why the Nazis had put us in there or what we had done wrong, but despite always trying to be co-operative with the Germans, things got worse. The ration cards were only issued to people who worked so there were no rations for women and children. They'd worked out the rations very carefully and it was enough to keep one person alive with a tiny bit spare, which was meant to cover any labouring the men had to do. If you could work full time, you earned enough money to buy a full week's ration of food, but for those of us they wouldn't let work, it meant, essentially, no food. You could buy the black-market food from The Thief if you had the money, but if you couldn't get work, the ration books were useless, as you had no money to buy the things legally.

It dawned on me why the first Romanies to be out on the field were so thin – they were slowly starving to death, however willing they were to work. My dad managed to get work most days because he had lots of skills, even electrical work which the Germans wanted. For anyone who could only do labouring work, it was terrible. They always needed electricians but they often needed no one for labouring or farm work as they had stacks of local people also competing for work.

I often wished we were back in the countryside where we could gather food from all around us from the fields and the woods.

One day, when Dad came back from work, he was carrying something in an old sack and he had a metal petrol can with him. My three brothers and I and Mum couldn't wait to see what he'd got – like a magician with a magic hat, he pulled out a one-ring stove which ran on paraffin and he had a whole can of paraffin – it had cost him four of our chickens on the black market but he reckoned that now, at least, we could cook so it meant we could buy potatoes and cook our own hens.

In the next few days, other people wanted to borrow our little stove, but dad always insisted that first, they had to provide their own paraffin. It led to arguments because more people wanted the stove than there was time for, but after a while, someone else managed to get their own stove in exchange for jewellery and one man did three days of work for a farmer for no pay to get a third one.

Even so, we none of us had enough food to eat. It was my brother Tarko who found us a solution, terrible though it turned out to be. There were several blackthorn bushes growing at one end of the field and an old hedge. Maybe it sounds silly, but I thought of them as being like our own barbed wire to keep the Germans out. Anyway, Tarko hit upon an idea to make money. I had a cheap necklace made up of glass beads which he begged from me on the promise that he would give me something in exchange later. Actually, I never expected anything, but I didn't need the necklace and he was so keen to have it that I gave it to him.

I watched what he was doing, curious as to his plan.

From the blackthorn, he ripped several long thorns, making sure he kept the spur on the end. Carefully, he shaved off the bark so it was light brown in colour. He'd found some old glue which dad had been intending to use for ages and on the spur of the thorn he put a dab of glue and then stuck a glass bead. I watched as he made several more.

The next morning when I got up, there was no sign of either Tarko or my younger brother Bas. Mum was worried about them, but Dad had to go to work so hadn't the time to be searching everywhere. I just thought they'd gone visiting to someone else's wagon.

At the end of the day, they had still not returned and Mum and I were getting worried, but in the early evening, just after dark and before dad got back, they suddenly appeared, breathless and carrying a sack.

They tipped the contents on the floor – bacon, eggs, a tiny bit of butter, cheese and a loaf of bread fresher than anything we'd seen for a long time.

"How did you? ..." Mum began.

They were bursting to tell us.

"We made hatpins and took them to exchange for food," Tarko explained.

"But no one's allowed to leave the camp," I said. "Who had food to spare here?"

"No one," grinned Bas. "We went into town."

"How did you get past the guards?" I asked, expecting them to say they paid a bribe.

"Over the wall, under the barbed wire," said Tarko, indicating the wall of the town with his thumb. "Ladies can't get metal hatpins and hairpins for love nor money these days. We did a roaring trade, swapping them for food."

"And what's more," added Bas, "We got two more bead necklaces, one for you," and he thrust one into my hand. "And one for us to make more."

Ten

The hatpin idea helped us a lot and everyone else, too. We ended up with surplus food which we gave to families or sold to wealthy neighbours at fair prices – unlike The Thief.

We were the only family selling things. The orders were strictly that no one could leave the camp except the official work parties of men and they were escorted to and from their work. Several more people tried to sell things to the guards at the gate or to those patrolling along the barbed wire fencing, but we had nothing to interest them, though they would buy bits of jewellery if the price was exceptionally low. We actually got a better deal – though not much better – exchanging anything like that with The Thief.

I and a couple of other girls made a little money or food offering to clean the boots of the soldiers on guard. They would come through the gate and stand with their backs to it, watching suspiciously whilst we worked. At first, they never took their eyes off us and I think they feared we were going to attack them (how with no weapons of any kind?) but at least it earned a little. I also used to take my fiddle and play near the gates and occasionally a guard would throw me a coin.

My brothers were the only ones who kept managing to get out of the camp, under the barbed wire on top of the town walls and dropping down the far side when they were convinced no one could see them. Then they'd wander into the town market and sell the hat and hair pins to anyone who'd buy. One of the local shops even bought a big stock of pins.

At first, they went a couple of times a week and when the blackthorn in the camp ran out of big thorns, they found more in other places on the edge of town and stripped them from there. Glass beads and glue could be bought.

They became familiar figures in the market place and as the demand for pins dropped they moved into crosses woven from willow and wooden flowers dipped in dye and pushed onto living hedge stalks but the pins were the big sellers always.

Meanwhile, work got scarcer and scarcer and my brothers' little market trading became more important. Many times, some of the senior men went to the German officer at the gate and pleaded to be given work so we could be fed, but the officer just said we were only there temporarily anyway and would soon be moving to somewhere with a lot of work to do.

Some of the families got sick because they had insufficient food. I'm not saying my family were well fed, but at least we did have something to eat. Dad wouldn't let us share with others any more, though it felt wrong not to especially when other peoples' kids were so thin and emaciated now. Dad said if we shared, we'd end up as bad as they were and we could see his point, though it was hard. There was resentment towards us and maybe someone tipped off the Germans about the brothers' business, I don't know.

One day at dusk, when the brothers were in the town trading, we heard two shots from over the far side of the wall. We wondered what was going on, then Bas suddenly appeared on the wall and half pushed half threw himself under the barbed wire and dropped to the ground. He had blood on him.

"They've shot Tarko," he wailed.

My parents and I and little Button, the youngest brother, ran over to him. He gabbled what had happened.

"The Germans, they were waiting for us when we came back. Just as Tarko was about to chuck the sack up to me on the wall, they fired. He was hit, he fell down, I couldn't help him. I saw a German aim at him and fire, then he aimed at me and I came down from the wall as quickly as I could. Hide me, hide me, they'll come for me."

Mum rushed him back to our wagon and I went too. When she checked, he hadn't been shot himself, but he was badly scratched from the barbed wire.

As she cleaned him, all he could say was, "They shot him, they shot him, Tarko."

Dad hadn't come back to the wagon with us but had gone to the gate. When it was dark you weren't allowed to go anywhere near the boundary fences or the town wall or the gate, but dad did. Now he came back.

He pulled mum into his arms. "I'm sorry, he's dead. They killed him." Mum gave a terrible wail and Button and I burst into tears. Poor Bas was already sobbing from his ordeal. "Other than saying he was dead, they wouldn't talk to me," dad said. "They say I have to go back in the morning and speak to the Herr Officer."

A couple of relatives from nearby wagons came in and asked what had happened. They were running a risk in curfew but mostly the Germans were quite relaxed as long as you didn't go near a fence. Dad explained and the relatives cried too.

That night, they did not come for Bas, but his nightmares were terrible to witness and we none of us had proper sleep.

Eleven

As soon as it was well light next morning, dad put on his one suit and he and I and I went to the gate. "I have come to see the Herr senior officer," he said.

The soldier looked at us through the gate and obviously thought about it for a moment, then he shrugged his shoulders. "Wait there," he said. He opened a box on a fencing post and took out a field telephone, ringing to the officer. We couldn't understand everything he said, but from his glances back, we worked it out. "Herr Hauptsturmfuhrer, a Gypsy begs permission to speak with you." The officer must have asked something. "The father of the kid that was shot," he continued.

We waited by the gate. After what seemed an age, an officer approached the gate and with him the junior officer, a sergeant and two ordinary soldiers with rifles over their backs. The officer looked us up and down through the gate and I felt as if he was gazing at us like we were dog droppings. Then my heart sank as I recognized who he was – the soldier who had treated Bavalengro so brutally. Bum Nose.

Dad said, "Sir, we ...."

Bum Nose shouted, "If you wish to address me, you will do it in the proper way, scum. The correct way is to say, Sir, please, sir, I request permission to speak."

"Sir, please, sir, I request permission to speak. My son ...."

"I haven't given you permission yet, fool," the officer shouted. "Ask again, properly."

I recognized it as a sort of bullying. He was trying to humiliate Dad and cow him. "Sir, please sir, I request permission to speak."

"Very well."

"Sir, yesterday ...."

"Sir, please, sir yesterday ...."

"Sir, please sir, yesterday the soldiers shot my son, I wondered why – I do not understand. And—"

"Why? You dare to ask why?" he shouted, louder than ever. "Your son was a criminal who broke curfew, and broke the rules of the camp by getting out, he sold property which I expect was stolen and you don't understand? Do you have mental problems?"

"Sir, please, sir, he was only twelve."

"Only twelve eh? Old enough for you to have taught him to disrespect the law. Let me tell you, Gyppo," and he waved a finger at Dad through the wiring in the fence. "You must have known what he was up to and told him to do it. I've a good mind to have you executed and the one that got away also. Doubtless he is another of your dirty little brats."

"No, sir, I—"

"Sir, please, sir, ignorant swine."

"Sir, please, sir, I did not tell him to do it, but we are all hungry, sir, and he was trying to help us."

He now seemed to ignore Dad totally. "Sergeant, assemble all the scum in the space over there so I can address them."

"Yes sir." The sergeant called through his megaphone. "All residents of the camp will come immediately to the space in front of the entry gate where the Herr Hauptsturmfuhrer wishes to make an important announcement. Come on, everyone, quickly now. Raus, raus, zack, zack." A few people left their wagons and several more peered out to see what was happening. "Raus, raus, zack, zack!"

It seemed people were being too slow for the Germans. "Give me your rifle," Bum Nose ordered one of the ordinary soldiers. The officer held the rifle so the barrel pointed up and pressed the trigger rapidly, firing three times.

Now people began leaving their wagons much more quickly.

"Raus, raus, zack, zack," the sergeant called again through the loud speaker.

Bum Nose raised the gun and took careful aim across the field. I went cold. He fired. I saw a wagon at the far side lurch as if it had been shot. Then everyone began to run towards the gate, parents grabbing children's hands, terrified. Near the front of the panting crowd, stood my dad and I, Kekkanav and Lon.

He took the sergeant's megaphone and gave him the gun in return.

"Now listen very carefully. You are not allowed to leave this camp unless you are a proper worker with escort. Anyone who does, knows now what will happen to them. We have no time for Gypsies and the presence of a few beggars who can play a musical instrument does not improve our feelings towards you. I can see the lucky boy who escaped last night and I am considering shooting him myself now. Rules will be obeyed. Orders will be obeyed without question. I hope I make myself clear? Now, where's that boy? Ah, I see him."

I turned to look but could not see Bas though I could see Mum with Button. No wonder he wanted to hide last night, I thought, my heart in my mouth.

Bum Nose's eyes swept round the gathered people. They settled on Dad and then switched to me.

"I know you from somewhere," he said. "Why is that?"

Twelve

"Please, sir, I clean boots, sir, for the Herr soldiers. Maybe it's—"

"No, something else." He looked at Kekkanav and Lon and gave a sinister smile of recognition. "Ah yes, of course, you were one of those present when these two fools said they could cure my horse. Well, gentlemen," he smiled at them. "Did you bury my horse properly when it died?"

"Sir, please, sir, yes, sir," replied Grandad Kekkanav in a gabble. I noticed for the first time that all his gold buttons from his jacket were missing and instead, I knew, The Thief and the soldiers would have them. In exchange, Grandpa had a piece of rope fastened round the once fine jacket to keep it closed.

"Well, I have a little job for horse buriers," he said, and gave Grandad a few very gentle slaps on his cheek. "Unteroffizier Maier," he called. A corporal stepped forward stood to attention and saluted.

"Sir?" he asked.

"Take these two Gyps and have them bury the dead donkey," he said.

"Sir," he replied and saluted again, then to Kekkanav and Lon, "You two follow me."

He led them from the camp, striding swiftly towards the town. "Now," said Bum Nose. "Fetch your blacking brushes; you can do my boots. Chair!" he called. "And, young woman, they tell me you can play the fiddle. You can play some old tunes for me." He shouted through his megaphone, "The rest of you go, and remember my words, go on, los, los."

I scuttled away and returned running with my boot black box and my fiddle and bow. He was seated on an old wooden dining chair just inside the gate. "Do the boots," he said.

I am good at tasks like that because I am meticulous and patient and it took me twenty minutes, by which time he had a pair of boots which all-but shone sunlight. I even cleaned and polished underneath.

"Good," he said. "Now play until the donkey buriers return."

"Sir, please, sir," I asked. "Is there anything the Herr Officer would like me to play please, sir?"

"You will know plenty of French airs, doubtless," he said.

"Yes, sir, quite a few," I replied.

"But I am German. Do you know any good German ones?"

I knew a few – as I said, we were often asked to play them by the occupation troops. I began with 'Deutschland Deutschland Uber Alles' which he clearly enjoyed and then 'Panzerlied' which was a favourite with the Panzers and 'Horst Wessel', which all the Germans seemed to like. "Do you know 'Marcha Erika'?" he asked. I thought I did, and took up the fiddle.

That was a real hit – it was like a signature tune of the SS. Bum Nose regularly slapped his knee to the beats of the drums which would have been in the gaps between the tune and such a smile crossed his face. "Gut, gut," he said. But my heart wasn't into happy tunes and I kept thinking of our dear dead Tarko. Without realizing what I was doing, I finished 'Marcha Erika' and moved into a hauntingly beautiful lament for my dear brother.

"Beautiful, beautiful," he said as I finished. "Play it again," so I did. I was on my third play of 'Deutschland Deutschland Uber Alles' when Grandad Kekkanav and Lon returned. They looked dirty, scratched and tired and carried a small sack with them.

"You can stop now," said the Herr Officer. "The donkey vets are back. You couldn't cure that one, could you?" he asked them. They just shook their heads. The guard opened the gates and let them in and the officer went out of the gate, leaving the chair behind him. I walked across the camp with them.

They were finding it hard to speak. "It was Tarky we had to bury," Lon said at last. "At the edge of the public cemetery. They said – they said the main cemetery was too good a place for a Gypsy brat so we had to clear out some brambles right on the edge and dig there. It was hard digging but he is at rest now. We asked for a priest, but the soldiers said no." They tipped out the sack. It contained bits of smashed bread and willow crosses. "We put one of the crosses on the grave."

I needn't have expressed my sorrow or that of Mum and Dad and Button because what the Nazis hadn't understood was that we were human like everyone else. What ate at us was not only the hunger, but the feeling of a terrible injustice, that we were being punished, not because we had done anything wrong but only because we were Gypsies.

You know now, of course, that our suffering had barely even started. I'm sorry, could I have a break now please?

Thirteen

During the next couple of weeks, Bum Nose sent for me to come and play for him at the gate almost every early evening. Meanwhile, our food situation got worse and worse and it was only the boot-blacking and the few coins I was thrown for the fiddling which kept any of us going.

One morning, about 8 a.m., we were summoned to the area by the main gate with the usual loudspeaker announcement.

"All residents will come immediately to the space in front of the entry gate for an important announcement. Come on, quickly now. Raus, raus, zack, zack."

The sergeant told us, "Tomorrow morning at 8 a.m. you will be moving. You will be entering temporary accommodation for a couple of days and will then be taken by train to a new camp in the east.

You will need no valuables with you since the Reich will provide all your needs. You will bring only what you can carry in one bag and the children five or over will be required to carry their bag for themselves. It is not a long walk, about five miles and you will all be given a very generous bread allowance which you can eat on the walk to your temporary hostel. That is all. Go and prepare."

One or two people tried task questions but they were ignored. We drifted back to our wagons and started to pack. Mum said, "If they think we're leaving what little money and jewellery we have left, they've another think coming. Why should we leave it for them to loot?"

We'd learned that the first Romanies to arrive on the field had been forced to hand over all gold and silver to the Germans which is why, when it came to trying to buy food from The Thief, they had so little. Throughout our weeks on the field, they had been the thinnest and the most ragged and they had lost more children through being too weak to face common illnesses than the rest of us. It was another of those things that made the injustice the greater.

Next morning, we were in the crowd at the gate by about 7.30. Early autumn approached and there was a light frost so that we huddled in our clothes – such as we still had. By now our clothes were beginning to get quite tatty. I know Foxy has explained about the sort of things his family wore, but we were a bit different, though still distinctive. When our men played for the gorjers – that means the non-Gypsy people – they wore suits, three-piece if possible and had on flat caps. For everyday use, the men were much more casual with any old trousers or shirt they could get – we usually begged our clothes. Today they were in their old suits and the women wore long colourful skirts like our Slovak cousins and usually white blouses and had shawls and head caps like Foxy's people or plain headscarves.

They marched us out of the camp in a long crocodile, guarded by several soldiers and gendarmes. We walked right through the town and as we did so, people even came up to us and spat at us and called insults at us. We did not know what we had done wrong to these people. I was pretty well in the middle of the column so I escaped the worst of it, though a stone did hit me a glancing blow.

At a large block of flats, we stopped. We were told all the second floor was ours. There was a long flight of stairs up to it, but those who could not walk, such as the elderly, were made to stand on one side. So, too, were very young children, the under-fives. The Germans said they could not be allowed to remain with their parents except for babies being breast fed but there was a kindergarten on the ground floor with trained nurses and teachers and they would be well looked after there and parents could visit every day. Old people who couldn't get up the stairs had to share one room on the ground floor.

Well, you could imagine how that went down with Gypsy people renowned for their devotion to their children. Everyone just refused, thinking the children were in danger. When someone asked why, one soldier said it was because there wasn't room for them and it might be dangerous with them possibly falling over the balconies. Then the Germans started to get annoyed and I feared they would start shooting or something, but it calmed down when a nurse came from the kindergarten and she was followed by a string of little children, most eating German chocolate. That soothed everyone. Another nurse trundled out babies in prams, three to a pram but all looking well. That was what did it. On the basis that the children seemed fine and they had been promised access every day, but still reluctantly, parents handed their little ones over. The old people were ushered into their separate part of the ground floor and we went, not without some trepidation, to the second floor.

Our new accommodation consisted of a series of small flats containing no furniture. I think there were almost thirty, all accessed from a balcony corridor. The problem was, there were several hundred of us and though all of us were related in an extended family, and to some extent related to the other groups, there were just too many people for those few rooms.

We had no bedding and were sleeping about ten or twelve to a room and people thought the under-fives were, indeed, far better where they were. We should have known the Nazis better.

Fourteen

Twice a day, drums of so-called soup and ersatz coffee were carried up to our floor and we learned that the Jews on the floors above us were fed similarly. Unless you could get some from the bottom of the drum, it was just grey coloured water. Very occasionally someone found a scrap of some sort of meat: more commonly, a piece of carrot or potato. With each serving, we were given a thickish slice of a peculiar bread which tasted coarse and the colour of which varied between grey and light brown.

The Jews had been on the floors above us about ten days, so far as we could tell. We were always hungry, but some of them had it worse because the very top floor only got bread if the Germans had managed to cut everyone else's bread at the right thickness, which was almost impossible. So, they often had no bread and when we ate ours we were very conscious that we were probably eating the bread which should have gone to a child, but we could do nothing about it.

Anyone who tried to ask a question or made any sort of a protest, however mild, was clubbed with a rifle butt. One of the women from a different Romany group from ours, spat over the balcony wall one day. I don't know if the spittle hit anyone but a soldier fired at her from below (but fortunately missed).

Visits by relatives to the children in the kindergarten were banned, despite the promise that had been made and the armed soldiers at the top of the stairs to our landing made sure no one could go down. Instead, mums and dads and older brothers and sisters had to content themselves with leaning over the wall of the walkway and shouting down to them. The Jews had to do exactly the same from their floors even higher up.

After we'd been there about ten days, things changed again. One morning, in mid-September 1942, lots of soldiers came rushing along our walkway, shouting and banging on doors.

"Raus, raus, schnell, schnell!" (Out, out, quickly, quickly!)

It rapidly became a scene of the wildest confusion. People were gathering their wretched belongings, plucking up babies and baggage amidst cries and shouts. Women wept, children wailed. We were frightened like horses with panthers in their midst as we struggled and huddled and pushed. Some had to be picked up and dragged by a relative, children were trampled on and all the time, the German soldiers at the doors shouting, "All out! All out! Clear this room. You're being moved to a different camp so we can get you idle scum to work." As we squeezed out of the doors, the soldiers kicked us and punched us to make us hurry.

From above, we could hear the clatter of feet and more shouting and soon lots of Jews came behind us, pushing and shoving as we all tried to get down the stairs at the same time. In the open, soldiers kicked us and it did not matter if they kicked children or old women. Those who fell and did not move fast enough were trampled.

Chased by soldiers, the nurses from the kindergarten placed babies on the ground or herded young children into groups and tried to get them to their own parents. The very old and those with disabilities were literally dragged from their ground floor part of the building. A few carts appeared and the soldiers heaved and pushed old people onto the carts, never gently.

Cruel chaos, merciless, raging and rampant, unbridled hatred turned on Gypsies and Jews for no reason we could understand. They shouted and pushed us into ranks of five and ordered us to follow the carts with the old people, terrified bawling children clutching their mothers' skirts, mothers clutching little babies, soldiers with their guns in their hands as if we were dangerous criminals seeking murder.

We shuffled for about three miles until we reached a railway line. Here were more soldiers, but calmer.

A long row of cattle trucks stood before us and at the front two steaming engines. The soldiers pushed and pointed, sending us Romanies to the back of the train and past lots of cattle trucks with a very large J or sometimes a Star of David chalked on. Some of the cattle trucks at the end, I think six, but I couldn't really count, had a single large letter Z in chalk. "Eile, eile" (hurry, hurry) the German soldiers shouted at us and pushed us towards the open truck doors. It was a big step from the ground into the truck so I stood back and helped old people, heaving them in when they couldn't step that high. I passed up little Button to Mum and Dad and was about to climb in myself when I heard a horribly familiar voice speaking in poor French. "Not that one." I turned and saw Bum-Nose watching me.

"You," he pointed with his whip. "Go and stand by the third carriage from the front and wait there until you are given permission to get in."

I must have looked puzzled. "Move", he shouted and struck me with the whip. I turned and saw Mum and Dad looking at me out of the door of the cattle truck then I turned and, clutching my fiddle and bow under my arm, jogged past the crowds of people struggling into Jewish trucks, right down the long length of the train until I reached the carriage he had told me.

Fifteen

I stood, frightened, and tried to look back to see my own family, but they were too far away or back from the truck doorways. My carriage was an old brown one, obviously once a dining car on the French railways. Two better carriages preceded it and there was another oldish one behind, then the rest of the train was cattle trucks.

I saw lots of people being driven non-too gently towards the train by soldiers I now knew as SS. If people broke away, they were beaten back. A group of obvious Jews had wild untrimmed beards, black curly locks at the sides of their faces, black hats and overcoats, their eyes red with fatigue and one or two – rabbis I suppose – fringed prayer shawls. The women and children were in old-fashioned clothes as if they had suddenly stepped from half a century before. They prayed aloud and sobbed as they shuffled and stumbled up into Jewish-star marked cattle trucks.

Everywhere, soldiers were sliding the doors shut and fastening them with clasps and metal spikes so they could not be opened from the inside. People peered out of glass-less windows which were covered with barbed wire.

Soldiers climbed up between the trucks, resting on covered ledges to protect them from rain; officers and NCOs wandered up the length of the train beside the track and clambered into one or other of the first two coaches; NCOs and a few soldiers entered the third and fourth carriages. As he passed me, Bum Nose saw me. He pointed to the third carriage and said, in his bad French, "You, get in there. You are the official entertainment." Four or five other prisoners, one wearing a brilliant white chef's hat, got into the same coach as myself. I did not know what to do. I wished I was with my family. I felt tears in my eyes.

The chef, Alphonse, put an arm round my shoulders and spoke to me – he was French. He explained that all of us were going to a work camp somewhere and not to worry because we would look after each other and he asked where my parents were. I told him and he looked grave. He said he'd been sent to do the cooking for the soldiers on the train and one of his colleagues (Daniel) was a French wine expert and two more were excellent cooks.

"You will do well for food," he promised me. "We shall eat the Germans' very best!" he whispered. "Worry no more, little violinist, at least you are not in a cattle truck," but actually I would have preferred to have been, with my family.

"Are you Jews?" I asked. He shook his head. "No, we are politicos – people the Nazis don't agree with as our politics are liberal, anti-Nazi and pro French. And you?" I didn't want to say because I thought he might be against Gypsies, so I pretended I hadn't heard as he was speaking very softly.

The train lurched and set off, slowly at first, carrying its heavy cargo of humanity.

The dining car had a kitchen and bar at one end and the rest of it was fitted with seats and dining tables. At the tables sat soldiers, a few officers and NCOs and the rest ordinary ones who, I learned later, were the off-duty ones.

They began shouting for food and wine and Jean, the third of the Frenchmen, who became my friend and helper, and a couple of others, bustled about bringing bottles of expensive wine and glasses and, soon after, the first of the food which Alphonse had cooked.

As they ate, Bum Nose, the officer from our camp, shouted down the carriage, "Oi, Gypsy, play your fiddle, you know the sort of tunes." So, I went through my full repertoire of German songs and followed it up with some Liszt, Brahms and some Wagner (which they loved) though not surprisingly the ones I was most ordered to play were 'Marcha Erika' and 'Horst Wesel'. They had me play from evening well into the night, by which time a good many Germans had fallen asleep. They told me to go into the fourth carriage and I could sleep there. I wondered about food, but as I passed the kitchen at the back of the coach, Alphonse waved me in and pushed a huge plate into my hands. I ate hungrily, but all the time wondered about my own family and what they had. Then all of us went through into the fourth coach which had a series of wooden seats. All the seats were taken – more politicos, said Alphonse, who knew several, but we lay on the floor or against the side of the swaying carriage, covering ourselves with coats and blankets which the politicos loaned us and I was quickly asleep.

Sixteen

We were awakened at dawn by banging and shouting and I realised that the train had stopped. We clustered at the windows and could see soldiers at every cattle truck, letting out single prisoners to empty slops buckets and take in buckets of water. My family was too far away to see any of them, but I did see two unfamiliar Gypsies.

The others were ordered to make breakfast but it was the wrong time of day for the fiddler so I stayed huddled in a corner. After about an hour, by which time the train had set off again, Jean came with a big hunk of bread plastered with thick butter and a cup of real coffee. He also passed on a few loaves to the politicos for them to share.

Most were French communists or socialists but there were a few gay men and a couple of French Jehovah's witnesses – all seemed to be nice people. I got chatting with a lovely lady called Maria and I told her about my family. She did not seem to be against Gypsies at all.

Alphonse and Jean plied me with coffee and croissants all morning: I had good roast duck early evening meal and soon after the train stopped again for another change-round of guards on the wagon fronts but the cattle trucks remained closed.

I had spent most of the day chatting to my new friend Maria. She'd attended Paris University where her husband was a lecturer, but he was killed very early in the war and they had no money. They had no family and she had become the concierge of a block of flats in Paris, but one day said something disparaging about the Germans and the next day was arrested by the Gestapo, tortured to reveal the names of conspirators (there weren't any) and put onto this train.

"But why haven't they put you and the other politicos into cattle trucks like the Gypsies and the Jews?" I asked.

She gave a faint smile.

"You have your own answer. We're not Jews or Gypsies. We are dangerous for our views but not our race."

I really didn't understand that. Now, of course, I do realize that the Nazis believed we and Jews were nicht menchliche – non-human.

"What will happen when we get to the work camp?" I asked.

"I don't know. They have had such camps for many years. From what I hear, you just have to work very hard."

"I've never been afraid to work – I'm a Gypsy," I said.

"Then you should be fine. There's a camp called Auschwitz with some nasty rumours about killing people, but we don't need to worry. I heard two of the guards talking and they said we were going to somewhere called Lublin, in Poland."

Maria had no children of her own and as I got to know her more and more much later when we were in the camp, I began to think of her like a surrogate mother and I felt very fortunate.

Anyway, about 8 p.m. on that first day, they sent for me to go back to the fiddling and I gave them another concert of about six hours non-stop playing before finally they let me go back to the politico carriage for some sleep.

I was again wakened early the next morning by the train juddering to a stop and the same sort of shouting I had heard on the day before. This time when they opened the doors of the cattle trucks to have a prisoner empty the slops, I could tell conditions had become much worse because the guards were holding their noses and putting cloths over their mouths and swigging a lot from hip flasks.

The day followed a similar pattern to the one before and I spent most of it in the company of Maria. I'd admitted the day before that I was a Romany and she was obviously interested and asked me lots of questions about me and my family and Gypsy life. She was such an intelligent woman and I really enjoyed our talks both on the train and after in the camp. The day ended as before with me being called to entertain until, finally, I was again allowed back into the politico coach to sleep. I did not see Bum Nose again.

Seventeen

It was mid-morning the next day before I woke up and only then because Jean was pushing me with his hand. "Wake up, wake up." He had buttered bread and coffee for me and I ate hungrily.

He spoke as I ate. "Apparently we are nearly at our destination and the guards are all excited and stirred up. Get your stuff together ready."

I peered from a door window and already the train was starting to slow down. For much of the time, there had only been our track, but now a second railway track ran alongside ours and gradually veered away.

When the train was down to little over walking pace, it rumbled past soldiers next to a large wooden gate on which I saw a sign in German (which I couldn't read), but also the name Majdanek, a name I had never heard before.

Moments later the train stopped. It was a small station consisting only of a platform. I could hear the soldiers leaving the carriages in front. The door opposite the one I had been looking from was thrown open and a guard shouted, "Out, out," to all of us. I held my fiddle firmly in one hand and my small bag of belongings in the other and was one of the first to jump down next to the train. An officer shouted at us in various languages and I understood that women had to go one way and men the other. I saw Alphonse, Jean and the others sent to a column of men whilst Maria joined me in a much smaller column of women. I peered down the train expecting to see the other trucks being opened and people pouring out, including my family, but it did not happen. Only the two cattle trucks next to ours were opened and those people were similarly directed to one or other column. I glanced back to see if my family or other Gypsies were leaving the train, but their cattle trucks remained closed.

An officer at the front of the column of men gave a big wave in the air and shouted something and the group of men trudged forward. Then a sergeant waved through the air and shouted at us and we followed. We were accompanied by perhaps half a dozen soldiers each armed with rifles. Whether they thought we really were dangerous I don't know but I now think it was done to cow us and frighten us. We came out of the little station into a narrow but deserted road and could now see that we were on the edge of a most beautiful town which I always thought was called

Majdanek but in fact it's real name was Lublin and Majdanek was the name the Germans had given it. It was good that they did because it meant that the true name was never polluted by what went on there. As we walked, I could see superbly designed stone and brick buildings with red tiled roofs. It looked almost like a toy town in the distance. We trudged along for perhaps three kilometres. Now and then I glanced back but I could no longer see the train though I did hear what I took to be people being shouted at to get off the train and the noise of train doors sliding open. Maria and I held hands wondering what was in store for us.

Finally, we reached a gate covered in barbed wire, which was swung open by two soldiers and we trudged through it, turning our backs to the road. After about five minutes, we stopped at a massive wooden and barbed wire gate which swung open. "In," the soldiers pointed. As we did, I turned a final time to see if I could see my family behind, but I could not. I never saw any of them again. I was grateful for Maria's hand. It gave me reassurance.

A sergeant spoke in French to us. "Stand to attention. Welcome to Majdanek, near the beautiful town of Lublin. Whilst you are here, you will be well looked after, but you will be expected to work and in exchange you will have comfortable accommodation and good food. This is the kapo who is the person in charge of your barracks and will take you to it shortly. There are rules in this camp. You will obey all rules at all times. Any attempt to escape will result in your being shot along with some of your friends to teach people that there is no escape from Majdanek. You are here to work for the Reich. All that matters now in your miserable lives is the Reich and your need to repay the Reich for its generosity in allowing you to live. You will repay that generosity by working hard – but work brings freedom. You will start work tomorrow. That is all."

He marched off along with the guards who had accompanied us out left through the barbed wire gate, leaving us under the tender mercies of our kapo.

"Right," she said. "You are all assigned to me and you will obey all my orders or," and she held aloft a thick stick of wood. "All guards will be addressed as 'Sir' and if you wish to speak you will say, 'Sir. Please sir, permission to speak', but only after I have given you permission first. You will stand at attention at all times when speaking to any guard. You will call me Frau Kapo or Ma'am and stand to attention whenever you speak to me. I will help you to remember for another time," and she slapped a woman, hard, across the face. "I hope that is all clear. Now follow me." One or two mumbled protests, but she glared at them and they shut up.

She set off at a trot, us following, passing several large wooden huts (or barracks as they insisted on calling them) until we reached one where she opened the door and went in. "Follow!" she ordered.

Eighteen

The hut into which we were ushered had a series of bunk beds in tiers of three down each side. The far end was already occupied by a lot of women, whom I gathered were all Polish, but very few of them were Jews and no Gypsies. We were allocated bunk beds at the end nearest the door, three to a bed and I was lucky in that Maria and I managed to get away with sharing just one bunk for the two of us.

Then the kapo ordered us out again and took us to another hut called the tailor's shop where we were ordered to strip out of our own clothes. Actually, there was a prisoner in there who whispered to Maria to hide her socks and undies under a seat to put back on later and so did I and we were very grateful to have them in the weeks ahead. They searched our clothes then searched our naked bodies in case we had jewellery hidden (but none had). They shaved our heads.

We all had the same uniform. There was a number on the front of the uniform which we each had to learn. I was prisoner 19191, an easy number to remember and Maria was 19190. The uniform looked like a pair of blue striped pyjamas except the cloth was coarser. We were also given boots – you had no choice of size, but fortunately mine were too big for me so I could stuff them with paper to fit later, but some people suffered terribly with boots too small for their feet.

Our first meal came at about 7 p.m. and consisted of odd looking and tasting soup, grey bread and ersatz coffee, like that we had experienced at Drancy. For mattresses, we had a pile of straw which looked to have been used by people before us.

We spent an uncomfortable night huddled together and in the morning, were roused at 5 a.m. by a siren and the kapo to go to roll call in the space near the entrance gate. There were hundreds of women and all had to be counted in their barrack blocks by their kapo – it was called *appell*. It took some time as one or two of the kapos seemed to find counting quite difficult. Then we were allowed to go for the usual soup, grey bread and ersatz coffee which this time they called breakfast. The claim about being well fed turned out to be another German joke. We got two meals in the camp and one in the factory and it was always the same and never sufficient, but we were lucky because those who did not work got only one so-called meal.

Throughout that first evening I wondered all the time about my family and where they were because I had hoped that the women might end up in the same part of the camp that I was. You were not allowed to leave the barracks so I could not try to see them, the only exception was to go to what they called the latrines, which consisted of a row of holes in boards and you balanced on the board to relieve yourself into the hole. You can imagine that the stench there was utterly terrible. You also had to be very careful because it was said that sometimes the guards, for sport, would throw a prisoner into a latrine. It was especially dangerous to go there at night because, although male soldiers rarely came into our compound, they did so at night, it was rumoured to find women out on their own in order to rape. If you were caught peeing in the hut, you got a terrible beating from the kapo so we had a sort of tin mug we all used and tipped out through cracks in the floor. The smell was awful but you got used to it.

Next day, on that first camp morning, all our barracks women were marched to the main gate of our compound where we were joined by armed soldiers and escorted back down the route we had taken the night before, across the railway line, across a piece of wasteland and thus to another railway line, which I realised was the branch line and which I had noticed on the way into the camp. Beyond that was a large factory. It was here that we were destined to work for the foreseeable future.

It was here, too, that I learned the fate of my own family. We were sewing leather. I had Maria sewing on one side of me and a Polish woman on the other. I recognized her as from our hut and asked her where she thought my family might be as I had not seen them since we got on the train. She looked at me pityingly.

"Poor child. Do you really not know?" I shook my head, worrying, suspecting something bad had happened. "I'm sorry," she said. "You will never see your family again in this life. They have all been murdered."

She went on to tell me the real purpose of the camp – to put to death large numbers of people and burn their bodies into ashes.

Yes, of course I mourned and wished I had died with them, but Maria was my constant strength in those awful early days of grief. I couldn't have got through without her.

Nineteen

The camp itself was divided into six compounds, but at that time only four were in use. Ours was compound One which was exclusively for women. In Two were male workers and in three was a sort of hospital for those who were sick, though it was made clear to me from the first day that I must never allow myself to appear ill, because being admitted to hospital was a death sentence. Now and then, they would clear the hospital by taking out the sick and shooting them.

The fourth compound was hell itself for the poor prisoners who were in there. I am not saying that it was easy for any of us, but our lives were heaven compared to the people in compound Four. They were all Russian prisoners of war who the Nazis regarded as only just human. Russian slaves had built the camp in the first place, but they had been allowed no places to sleep and given food even more minimal than ours.

They had to dig holes in the ground to live in to keep out of the bad weather, but by the end of their first winter all but a handful of the 10,000 had died. We hardly saw those prisoners because they were too far away, but from what we'd gathered they were living skeletons of rags who were not destined to live very long at all.

In the days that followed I learned more about the Polish women, most of whom were politicos who were considered dangerous because they were largely educated and could think for themselves. I got on well with most of them, but you had to be careful what you said to anyone as the Nazis rewarded people who told them scandal or what they deemed threats.

The huts where we lived and slept – the Germans insisted on calling them accommodation blocks as if they were luxuries, but between themselves called them barracks – were each designed to hold about 700 people. The one entrance door at the end had a room to the right which was the Kapo's private room with a bed and a little desk and her own food supply. The Kapos were often violent people brought from prisons, not actual SS, and they issued us with our orders. Ours was a Polish woman who had been serving a sentence for murder and was given her job at Majdanek so that she was still locked up, but in the view of the Nazis was doing something useful. Opposite the Kapo's room, an open space on the wooden floor, was where some of the prisoners chose to sleep or where they slumped down if they were too ill to reach their own bed. Mine and Maria's bed was two tiers on from that.

Though the hut was crowded, it did help you to keep warm in a shed which had gaps in the walls through which the winds came. Skylight windows let in light, but the Kapo had an actual window.

Every morning the siren went off in the camp at about 5 a.m. and the Kapo came down the aisle between the bunk beds banging a lump of wood on the frames to get people up quickly. Slow ones got the club on their legs or arms. We had to run out and stand in our ranks for the *appell* (counting); if all was well, breakfast was next, in tin bowls which you had to eat quickly, and then in the same bowl get the ersatz coffee. Most people saved their bit of bread to eat later.

The factory lay to the south of the town and we began work at 6 a.m. prompt where they were making light armoured cars for the German army. Compared with work in the camp, which in one way or another was being forced to help the Germans to murder people in the gas and carbon monoxide chambers, the factory wasn't too bad. Most of the parts of the vehicles were made elsewhere except for the larger pieces of steel sides, bottom chassis and top which were made in a separate building. Maria and I mainly sewed the leather for the seats, a job which made my fingers very sore until they got hardened, due to having to force the thick needles through the leather. When I wasn't doing that, I was assigned to drilling holes through the metal plates for the rivets and bolts of the assembly.

As the weather got colder and autumn progressed, we were glad to be inside. One place we none of us wanted to work was in the paint shop because people paint-sprayed and there was no protection. You breathed in metallic paint all day long and we knew it was lead based. People there eventually became too ill to work with clogged up lungs or poisoned systems and that was when they were selected to die. Being sent to work there was a sentence of death.

The only exception to work inside was when a train arrived on the sidings by the factory and we were then all ordered to leave our work to unload the train of all the parts needed for the vehicles – engine components, wheels, tyres, guns, headlamps, wires and so on.

That outside work was what gave me the idea of how to escape, because at the far side of the sidings was a pine fence and beyond it a forest. I had no idea what lay beyond the forest, but I just wanted to get away and find any of my distant relatives who were still alive in France. It drove me on, that and the memory of my own family and their awful fate. I wanted to beat the system somehow and escape was all I could do for that aim.

Twenty

One day, standing to attention at roll call, I watched the wind play on a bit of rag, throwing it up and then down so it caught against the corner of a hut. It struggled and flapped, trying to get free whilst the wind teased it and pretended it would let it go at any moment. I thought the rag was like me, caught, with the guards teasing me into thinking that one day I might go free again, but if so only as a torn and useless former human being.

The following morning, the rag was still there. It had ceased violently trying to attract my attention, but was now flapping up and down, as if beckoning to me. There was little breeze yet that rag moved of its own accord or through some hidden magic force which had entered it and given it impetus. Then it dawned on me what it really was – a vurmi!

Vurmis are Gypsy signs. We all use them when we are travelling and there are lots of different ones.

Some families use only their own so that distant relatives know which Gypsies are going where. Others are used by almost everyone and one of those is a bit of rag tied in a tree to say, 'we have gone this way'. But they have lots of deeper meanings as some vurmis will tell you who the Gypsies are or will mark a special place, perhaps where a loved one is buried or give a warning about police or gamekeepers.

It seemed to me that this vurmi was especially for me. Apart from it being a traditional sign, Vurmi was the nickname of my aunt – you remember – the one who was making the medicinal mash for the horse. After all, there were no more Gypsies in the lines of shabby blue and once-white striped uniforms, their heads hanging in fatigue and fear, so it could only be a sign from Aunt or from more of my dead family. Only I knew it as a Gypsy sign and as I furtively watched it, I became more and more certain that it was a vurmi especially for me, trying to get me to follow.

To follow? From the corner of a hut? To where? How? I thought of that grey room in the flats where we had last been all together. I felt a knot of hatred and anger against the people who had done this to us and so cruelly, so undeservedly. That strengthened my resolve and made me more determined that, somehow, I must escape.

Escape? The very thought was terrifying. I had seen what happened to a Polish woman who escaped and was brought back – we had all been made to watch. The night before, she had been put into a cage with bars like an animal. Next day we were ordered to parade in our blocks and stand to attention as the woman was brought from the cage. A sign was hung round her neck: 'Yippee! I'm back!' it declared in Polish in large letters. They dragged her to where her block stood at attention and she had to pick two friends to accompany her. The condemned woman did not refuse the order because if she did, she had been told that the alternative was ten women picked by the junior officer. The officer made a sarcastic speech to everyone, expressing sorrow and disappointment that she had hurt everyone's feelings so badly by not loving us all any more and wanting to leave us so selfishly. He finished his vicious mockery with a warning: no one escaped from the camp, everyone was recaptured, innocent people had to suffer in consequence. Finally, the three were forced to run between a double line of soldiers armed with rifle butts and clubs and whips and they were beaten until they emerged, barely alive, at the far end of the 'naughty tunnel' where they were finally clubbed to death.

I often wondered what I would do – who would I pick to die with me from my block? How could I pick Maria? There were no other Gypsies, but I might not have picked them anyway. I suppose I would have ended up picking Maria and another woman I liked in the hope that we went on to a better place together. No, I was wrong – it would have to have been other Gypsies had there been any. It was a dilemma that gripped me now as we made our routine march to work.

When chance allowed, when there were no listening ears, I told Maria of my proposal, but added that I feared it would lose her life for her if I did.

"Only if you get caught," she reassured me. "And if you are, you are like a daughter to me and I would rather die with you than on my own. But you have to plan it and plan it so well that you cannot be caught, or, if you are, that you have a means of killing yourself."

"Come with me," I said.

"Oh no, that would never do. You are young and able to run fast and hide. I am too old and would just hold you up and increase your danger. Just promise me you won't get caught."

I put that promise into the steel of my soul. Not taking her was hard, but I knew she was right and between us we began preparations for my attempt at freedom.

Twenty-One

Maria and I often talked about what sort of things I would need to have with me in order to get away and above all, to survive thereafter.

Escape from the actual camp was almost impossible because of the high fences, which were electrified, the barbed wire, the patrolling soldiers and the soldiers with dogs trained to attack anyone they were ordered to.

It seemed to me that the best place to escape from would be the factory. It was built alongside the branch line, but beyond it lay the trees where I was sure I would be able to move without being seen, though I had no intention of staying in the wood and hiding because they would obviously send guards to search there for me and the result would be the terrible fate for me and for Maria and for someone else, which I feared so greatly. Another thing which upset me was knowing that I could not take my fiddle with me.

The first priority was food and with Maria's generosity, we began saving a little of both our bread rations every day from the factory. When we got our factory bread, we switched it with some of the oldest and stalest hidden food. It was impossible to smuggle anything back into the camp because spot searches were often undertaken and anyone found with illicit goods was severely punished. We therefore contrived to make a small, very secret, store place in the factory. We had no belongings of our own which we could access in the factory, but needles were kept in boxes and we took one of the boxes and hid things in the bottom, putting a thick layer of needles on the top. There were shelves where the boxes of needles were kept and we put that box underneath several others. We had no fear of discovery as long as we were careful because only women working on the leather sewing had access to those needles.

My second priority was for a good sharp knife. Having a knife in one's possession was always a capital offence resulting in shooting or hanging by the guards. Knives were unheard of in our part of the factory – the Germans were paranoid – but I had noticed that whilst we slaves ate our meagre soup and bread and ersatz coffee at lunchtime, most of the guards went into a separate room where they had metal knives forks and spoons for their far more luxurious lunches which were made by professional cooks. On those occasions, there would sometimes be visiting SS and they would then pick a few prisoners randomly to work as waitresses.

One day, just before we were due to resume work, I went to the guards' dining room, knocked and reported that I had been instructed to collect up the dirty plates and to take them to the kitchen because the kitchen had a problem and were short staffed. I took a pile and set off for the kitchen, on the way secreting a knife and fork and spoon in my clothing. The guards took almost no notice of me and just left me to get on with the clearing up. They never questioned whether I should have been there. I went into the kitchen and just put the plates down and left. A quick glance told me that neither Alphonse nor Jean were there, so I don't know what happened to them. The cutlery went into the needle box whilst we worked out how we might get the knife sharpened without getting caught. Only later I realised how fortunate I had been to get away with such a plan, but I reasoned that had I thought it through more thoroughly, I would have looked more scared and given myself away.

Actually, I believe Maria never knew why I wanted a knife – not simply to help me to escape and keep free, but so that if I had been caught I had every intention of falling on the knife before they could capture me.

Twenty-Two

One of the work bays in the factory contained tools to repair machines or to sharpen implements and in there was a woman from our barracks with access to a grinding wheel. It was very dangerous to ask other prisoners for help because if they betrayed a plot to the SS, they were rewarded with extra food or privileges, but Maria took the risk with this woman whom she had known before their arrests and asked her to sharpen the knife. She gave no reason, but hinted it was because someone wanted to kill themselves with it so it needed to be sharp. Prisoners often killed themselves, though usually by throwing themselves onto the electrified wires. The suffering of some of the Russian prisoners and some of the Jewish men was so terrible that they sometimes sought their own drastic way to freedom.

We could tell when a supply train was due because we began to get short of materials. One day, back in the barracks, I told Maria that if at all possible I would escape next time a train came as by then I had a good stock of bread.

I did not have long to wait. Two days later we were ordered to go out and help to unload a train. I retrieved the bread and the now sharp knife with its fork and spoon (why a fork? I really don't know! I think it was because you had so little in the camp and nothing of your own that it seemed like a good idea.) With them stuffed under a vest I trotted out behind Maria to unload when two women in the leather shop stopped me. "Here," they said. "Take this." They had made a leather jacket and told me to take off my pyjama style jacket and put the hand-made leather one on underneath. "It will help you keep warm," one said. "Good luck, Godspeed and tell the world what is happening," she added.

I was a little frightened because had I been seen we would all have been executed, but that surety gave me the confidence that they were not about to betray me.

" Thank you," I whispered. "Remain with God."

I don't know to this day whether they had made the jacket specially for me, but doing something in the factory you weren't allowed to do was a sort of act of defiance and hope, so maybe that's why. Or maybe they just liked me. At any rate, they must have known about the intended escape.

We trotted to the train and began hauling off the various parts, carrying larger and heavier ones. Maria and the women who had given me the coat clustered round me pretending to unload so the guards could not see me very well and Maria said, "When I say 'Now', get under the train. Good luck, God be with you."

"Now!"

I dived between the bottom of the train and the track and squatted underneath one of the trucks, waiting until I was as sure as I could be that it was safe to continue. Had a guard found me there, I planned to say that I had gone there for a wee, as there were no latrines for the prisoners in the factory.

When no one raised the alarm, I crept to the opposite side of the truck and cautiously stuck my head out. I could see no guards at all on this side, but I could not be sure there were none on the roof of the train. When one came in at the other sidings loaded with people to be killed, there were always SS with machine guns in case anyone made a run for it, but I reasoned that there was no need to have guards on the top of a goods train carrying materials.

I plucked up courage, said a prayer to God to help me, burst out from under the train and ran. I dared not look back. At any moment, I expected the click of a safety catch of a rifle and the single shot which, I knew, would hit me in the leg to fell me and allow them to recapture me alive ready for their bit of fun.

Under my jacket and leather coat I clutched the knife ready to plunge it into me if that happened.

Ahead of me was the pine fence. I reached it, grasped the top and half vaulted, half climbed over. As I touched the ground I was sure this was when the bullet would come, when (they imagined) I would be thinking I had actually got away. I ran across the open space, weaving this way and that. Why didn't they hurry up? Shooting as I landed over the fence was when any sadist guard would prefer, but there had been no shot. I weaved in and out of the first of the trees, expecting the shot or at the very least the following footsteps. My chest seemed stretched beyond life for all the gasping of air I had done, my legs were tired and I could run no more. I decided that the best thing would simply be to stop and face them. At least giving myself up and then killing myself would take some of their fun away. I turned, stood resolutely and looked.

There was no one there.

No guard, no sharp shooter, no one.

Was this part of their joke? I wasn't sure, but I slipped into the trees and began alternately running and walking to get as far away from hell as fast as possible.

Twenty-Three

I walked for several hours through the forest, trying as far as I could judge from the sun to travel south and west. My ears and eyes strained for any pursuit, but as the time passed, I became more and more confident that I had truly escaped. I changed my jackets over so that the leather one was on top of the blue striped but my trousers were still the stripy ones so I mudded them to disguise the fact. I thought that if a local person saw me in prison garb they would realize and then probably betray me. Any people who did that were well rewarded by the Nazis.

As dusk fell, I allowed myself some bread and a good drink of water from a stream and then huddled against a tree trunk, pulling leaves and dry vegetation round me for warmth.

Romany people can survive well in a rural place because they know all the edible natural foods – as Foxy has already described. So, though I cannot claim that my diet was rich, in the days which followed, it certainly improved on that of the camp. It consisted mainly of nuts and whatever fruit I could find, plus herbs. The only problem was I could not light a fire to cook anything which limited me. I had already decided to be vegetarian, even though in the camp you had no option but to eat the peculiar stuff they called soup which sometimes had a smidgeon of unidentifiable meat in. I saw meat as belonging to some animal which had been killed and I'd seen enough brutal killing to last me forever. I wouldn't even take fish from the streams, even though I knew how to, or eggs from nests though I did sometimes take hens' eggs and, once, a huge cheese, from the occasional farm I passed.

I tried to move south and west, especially west, in the hope of getting back to France and finding relatives, but had no compass or maps so relied totally on the sun.

It was not a large wood and mid-morning of the second day, I reached the edge and saw ahead of me rolling hills where the horizon seemed to stretch before me forever like a symbol of my own freedom reaching ahead.

As I moved into the hills, ever cautiously, there were fewer hiding places if anyone was about and food was not as plentiful, but I managed eating the stored bread when I could find nothing better. Here and there were tiny farms which I skirted except once, one early morning, when I found a nanny goat which obligingly let me get some of its milk spurted straight into my mouth.

By now, I knew that my absence would have been missed at *appell* but I wasn't too worried about Maria being discovered as my helper as in our hut, we women got on well and it was to no one's huge advantage to betray her, get a reward and be rewarded even more with the curses and hatred of everyone else in the barracks.

On the fifth day, I found myself on lower ground which had several small farms. At one of these, I sneaked into a barn and took a dozen eggs and a pile of corn, which I carried in an old sack I found there and I also took a second sack from which I ripped out the bottom to use as a short skirt over my striped trousers.

The whole time I was in that low-lying area I felt in danger because, although it was countryside, there were more people about, though I never saw any soldiers.

Day six saw me back in the hills and feeling the need for a bit more thieving. You may say stealing is wrong, but this was a question of survival, not greed. I sneaked into a farm looking for hens' eggs and instead found three heavy and beautiful cheeses in an outbuilding. I only took one to keep me going and a good job I did as that range of hills took a full week of walking with little to find in the wild. I thought that if I ever became rich, I'd find this farm and pay for the cheese because I'm sure my taking it must have caused hardship to someone.

I did not know it, but I was getting near the end of my journey. When I moved out of the hills, they ascended onto a range of most picturesque mountains. They were bleak and cold, with early winter snow on the peaks, and food was difficult but I managed, thanks in no small part to that cheese.

I left the mountains on the lower slopes, entering a large and thick forest. Here and there were paths, but I was still trying to get south and west. Almost the first important thing I saw was a vurmi, a Gypsy trail sign of a bit of rag tied in a bush next to a path and that gave me huge hope because though it looked old, I knew that somewhere were Gypsies, my own people.

Twenty-Four

For the past few days I had been aware that though I was successfully walking south, the west was eluding me. It was just that there hardly any pathways or tracks to the west, only south; the one with the vurmi was also south or so I judged from the sun.

It was not a huge wood, though larger than the one near the camp. I walked for the rest of the day, feeding on handfuls of herbs and the last of the cheese. I also found fresh nuts on the ground – filberts – from this year – which I saved for the next day along with four gold-brown fruit from a wild apple tree.

Soon after mid-day, the trees of the forest grew thinner and I knew I would be leaving it shortly. Ahead of me, at the last of the trees, I saw below a large lake, probably a kilometre away. I was a little concerned about going into the open. I could see no cover near the lake and at the far end there seemed to be a couple of men fishing with rods. Right at the finish of the path I had taken through the wood, I found another vurmi and this was what gave me the courage and hope to continue.

It was a double vurmi with a piece of flowery red cloth tied to a twig and impaled on several thorns. Wrapped in its middle, so it stood out from one end, I saw a twig, carefully sharpened and then disguised with earth so the sharpening was not obvious. I recognized it immediately – 'Gypsies ahead, go straight on.'

But ahead was the lake, though on the slopes at the far side stood another wood. So whichever Gypsies had left it meant anyone who came to re-enter the wood at the far side. I marked in my mind the spot the stick pointed to, near a row of pine trees. Of course, I couldn't actually cross the lake so I chose the end where there were no anglers, walked down the slope and set off to walk round the edge of the lake to reach the far side. At one place, I had to paddle through a wide stream feeding the lake, its bed comprising many medium and small stones of varying hues, all rounded by the effect of the running water. If the fisher people at the far end saw me, they could not have recognized concentration camp trousers at that distance, muddied and disguised, and I suspect they would have been far more interested in the fish.

It took me almost two hours to walk round the loop of the lake and if I hadn't been a prisoner on the run I would have enjoyed it as a leisurely stroll in the warm sun, but I constantly had to be conscious of the danger from soldiers or people who might betray me.

I climbed the slope towards the row of pines, all the time searching for more vurmi. Vurmi don't have to be tied into a tree or a bush, they can be on the ground, or be part of the old ashes of a Romany fire. I could see none until I had gone right up the slope almost to the trees when I found something strange. It consisted of a long mound in which grass and little weeds were beginning to show through a carpet of pine needles. It had to be man-made, but I couldn't see a purpose to it. It seemed to have been put there deliberately to overlook the lake and I could see no paths on into the forest at the far side of it until I came to its end. There I found two things, one of which I did not understand.

Where the mound ended, was an odd vurmi. It consisted of four rounded stones, obviously from the stream bed. One was medium sized and dark, another medium and light, and two more smaller, one dark and one light and all four had been pressed into the mound in a simple row to make them look as if they might be there by chance. It meant Gypsy families, but told me nothing else.

Several Gypsy groups use vurmi like those to identify who they are, sizes and colours of stones showing a rough idea of how many people there were and their sexes. Usually there'd be another vurmi, like a tuft of horse's hair apparently caught under the edge of a stone if they were Lovari or an old rough scrap of metal if they were Kalderash, but these stones were silent.

Next to the end of the mound I saw a path, hardly used, but at whose entrance was another clear vurmi – a piece of the same cloth as at the other side of the lake. I was sure now that I must be near other Romany people, so as I walked along the path, my heart joyous, I whistled an old Romany tune.

Suddenly, someone grabbed me from behind, holding me tightly. I did not understand what the young man was saying but I knew the meaning of the knife at my throat – "One wrong move and your throat is slit."

THE
TOGETHER
TESTIMONY

One – Zuzzi

The person holding me was very strong and muscular and I knew I could not break free. He spoke very sharply to me, but I did not understand him. I guessed he wanted to know what I was doing there, but of course I could not say anything about escaping from the camp. I said, "I mean no harm," speaking in French. I felt his muscles relax just a fraction as if, he thought, I was not quite as dangerous as he feared. Slowly, he turned me round to face him and put the point of the knife at my neck so it pricked me. I looked at him very carefully. It took no imagination on my part to believe that I was looking into the face of a Romany. He must have thought the same.

"Tu Romi?" he asked.

I nodded my eyes up and down because I couldn't nod my head with the knife resting there. "Ava," I said. He relaxed his grip on me even more now and gazed into my eyes.

I said something in Romany then repeated it, as he couldn't work out my words. I swore under my breath in Romany which he did understand as I felt him relax still further and he took the knife from my throat.

"Who are you?" he asked in Romany. "What is your name?"

"Zuzzi," I answered. "I'm on the run. Please help me."

He let go of me totally and pushed the knife back into his belt. "Who are you on the run from? What are you doing here? How did you know I was here?"

I shook my head. "I didn't, but I saw the vurmi. I was trying to get back to France going south and west but especially more to the west to try and find if I had any family there still. They killed most of my family in a concentration camp."

He was more relaxed still and suddenly the tables were turned. Now he could find out what a knife at his throat was like – I pulled my dagger from my belt and put the prick of it against his throat. "Now it's your turn to answer my questions."

"Okay, okay," he said. "You don't need the knife. I'm on the run, too. I saw the Nazis kill some of my family and the rest I know they have murdered and buried in the wood. It looks like we are both in the same sort of mess. I've a hiding place just near here, let's go there and I can give you some food and we can talk and you can rest there safely."

From then on, we talked in Romany. Our dialects were not quite the same but close enough for us to be able to understand each other. He was excited and so was I. "Where are the others?" I asked. "I saw the vurmi." A grey shadow seemed to fall over his face.

"Dead," he said. I nodded now that the knife had been withdrawn.

"Mine, too," I said. "Murdered by the Germans."

This time it was his turn to nod his head. "I have been hiding here in the forest for some time," he said. "My place is not easy to spot and I think we will both be safe there. Come, I will take you."

I walked beside him studying him as I did. He was a little taller than me and very scruffy looking with black tousled hair. His clothes were all shabby and torn but having said that I don't suppose I looked much better to him.

He led me along several tracks, all the time talking quietly and that's how I answered him. Finally, we came to a part of the wood where the trees were not quite so close together and where they stood back a little from quite a broad track on which I could see vague traces of wheel marks. He pointed towards an array of thorn bushes. "There!" he said. Old branches were littered all over the ground and he picked some up and moved them to one side to reveal a narrow path. As we went along, he put the branches and twigs back behind us. Finally, we reached a hole underneath a blackthorn bush. He signalled me to follow and crawled through it. At the far side was the clearing that was to become so familiar to me as my home, my refuge and my hope of life to come. There was a rough traditional Gypsy shelter made of branches and canvas and near it the ashes of the fire. "Only at night," he said, pointing at the ashes. "In the day, someone could see smoke. Oh, and there is one more thing," he said. "I have seen terrible things and now I cannot face seeing meat because of the suffering of the animals, so I'm sorry, but you will get no meat here unless you get it yourself."

I nodded, "Me too," I said. "I am now very against eating meat and I've vowed that I will never do so."

"Foxy," he said pointing to himself and I responded, "Zuzzi."

He poured and passed me a beaker of some sort of home-made alcoholic sloe drink which was utterly delicious and just what I needed after a long walk through woods in a situation which could have been so dangerous. And then we sat by the remains of the last fire and told each other our life histories and the traumas and sufferings we had both experienced and our hopes for a life of freedom in the future and above all justice for Gypsies. We each cried several times like little children and hugged each other and told what we had witnessed and happened to us.

As dusk fell and turned to darkness, Foxy lit the fire and soon there was a pot of vegetables and hazel cakes fried in vegetable oils which proved to be delicious after my long and tiring journey. When we were tired, he took me through into the little shelter and gave me his blankets so that I could lie at the back and huddle against his back as he lay across the entrance. "We will have to make this shelter a lot bigger," was the last thing I remember him saying to me before deep sleep overcame me.

Two – Foxy

We slept until stars faded and grey dawn broke and the next morning, I took her hand and led her down the track back to the main woodland path, covering our trail once again with the branches. We crossed over and followed the vurmi that were very familiar to me to get to the site of the old camp where my family had been. I asked her to look round and see if there was anything of use.

Earlier, over a cold but welcome breakfast, she'd explained that the main thing she wanted was more clothes because those she was wearing had not been changed since leaving Majdanek. Believe me, she was also in need of a massive wash. We have a belief, we Gypsies, that you should avoid wearing the clothes of dead people because it is unlucky and it can bring their spirits to haunt us. There were lots of women's clothes in the remains of the wagons and I admit I tried to tempt her to take some, but in the end, she limited herself to curtains, blankets and any other pieces of cloth she could find and also several sewing packs so she could make clothes of her own without breaking the tradition. I gathered up more canvas in order to enlarge our tent and also a few tins of food but I'd removed most of those already. She was itching to have her new clothes so she could put them on instead of the old camp ones and wash away the dirt of cruelty and oppression.

An old dog watched us. Zuzzi crouched down beside one of the wagons and it shuffled to her, she stroked its head and it looked relieved to have found a person. "Shall we take the dog with us?" she asked.

"No," I shook my head, "The presence of a dog could give us away. Anyway, I've seen it before and it seems to be coping here OK."

We packed the things we had found into looped sacks made from old blankets. She gave the dog one last fondle, and we set off back to the hideaway. The next day we went hunting the woods for food and in particular for nuts of which there were a great many, even though it was late autumn. Some of the animals and birds obviously relied on them, but there seemed to be plenty to go round.

This was pretty much our pattern for the next few days except on one day, because I'd discovered Zuzzi's wealth of medical knowledge, I took her to Uncle Vanta's old place and she was able to find a treasure trove of medicines and medical equipment which she was sure would come in handy.

She called our camp in the thorned enclosure 'Thorn Castle', our fortress against racist killers.

I suppose at first, I was a little cautious of Zuzzi because although she was a fellow Romany I had been on my own for some time and I was a little anxious about how I should behave in the presence of a young woman. There are what I suppose you'd call taboos or rules you have to live by before you marry. I was worried, too, about getting attached to her after what had happened to my lovely friends at the hands of the Germans. I could not face another heartbreak.

I can't claim that our breakfasts were ever anything special but I did my best by making hazel bread and grinding up extra acorns and bits of fruit to go in it. From time to time I'd liberated flour from barns, making it look like a bag had burst so no one knew any was missing and although the resulting bread was heavy, it was food. As I say, we could not light the fire during the day or I would have cooked them in a little grease but we used to have this for breakfast, cold from the previous night and only in the evening when it was dark would light the fire and have a cooked meal.

One evening, when we were sitting by the fire in the dark, safe in the knowledge that no one could see either our fire or the smoke coming off it – though I suppose someone nearby could have smelt it – Zuzzi gave a great sigh.

"You remember I told you how I used to play the fiddle for our people and then for the Germans. Really, it was the fiddle which saved my life, but I could not bring it with me out of the camp. I wish I had one now. I could play the smell of the fire, the light of the stars and the moon, the warmth of the sun, the sound of the birds, the sight and sound of the animals and of love and hope. But I have no fiddle now."

Three – Zuzzi

Foxy thought for a moment, then said, "Maybe I can get one. There used to be one or two fiddles in the old camp, but I haven't noticed them on the times I've been there. They must be in people's wagons, but it seems somehow very unlucky to be going into a wagon of someone who has died so terribly. Uncle Vanta was a very good fiddler. He seemed to be able to play anything on it, but of course he used to pretend to be a fool. That way, people paid him more through astonishment at what he could actually achieve with a bow and fiddle and at his joyful and joking way in playing it, alternated with the most profound pieces imaginable. I wonder what happened to his? Do you think it would be unlucky to take his? I don't even know if it's still there. I'm sure he wouldn't mind."

I was sure, too. We found Vanta's violin, a musical coffin, lifeless as the now well-rotted Dog, on the ground. I imagined Uncle Vanta's spirit somewhere out there in the forest – maybe he would hear my music, but at the thought of him tears came into my eyes. Foxy put an arm round me and pulled me to him – he had tears of the same thoughts.

I picked up the fiddle full of hope, but found that it was broken – it felt a blow to my hope. I could only guess how it had got broken and I surmised it may have been knocked from somewhere; perhaps even from Uncle Vanta's own hands, and then some big footed Nazi had stood on it. At first, I thought the damage terminal, but when I looked more closely saw that it was in fact the neck that had been snapped.

Foxy said that one of his uncle's boxes was for violin maintenance and sure enough, it lay underneath the cart. I put it under my arm, checking first and finding the contents included a violin knife, varnish and spare strings.

"Come on," I said. "Let's see if we can make it into a fiddle fit for a Romany virtuoso." On the way back, Foxy noticed a tree he'd never spotted before, perhaps because it wasn't the height of most of the nearby ones. What drew me to it was its type – maple – which I knew was the preferred wood for the neck, so Foxy cut off a branch he thought would be of the right thickness and length and then, in his usual way, disguised the cut on the tree with earth so it did not look recent. Back at the clearing, I inspected both the instrument and the wood and approved. I thought it would not look much of an instrument with a rough replacement neck and it might affect tone. I suspected

I was a far better player than he, but I reckoned he had the edge when it came to actually making a fiddle neck.

There and then he set to, first peeling the bark off and then gradually whittling the wood to get the right shape of neck, or as near to the original as he could. It took several days, off and on, until he was satisfied, but I declared it not quite the right shape and it took many more days before I was satisfied. Then it was a case of gluing it to the sound box. Finally, he gave it a coat of varnish. It wasn't seasoned wood so he kept another piece of maple to weather and age for a replacement neck in the future.

To be safe, he left it two or three days to ensure that the glue and varnish was properly dry and all the time I was itching to test it, but when he was sure it was okay, he put back the pegs and strung it.

I couldn't wait to try it. I picked it up, held the bow aloft, and was about to give it a huge burst of sound when Foxy stopped me. "Zuzzi," he panicked, "The sound of a fiddle can go a long way in the forest and if the wrong people hear it they will know that Gypsies are here."

I felt very crestfallen and then said, "Oh very well, I will wait until it is dark."

"Then do try to play it quietly," he said. I gave him a look until he looked ashamed, but, that night, I curled the notes from the fiddle, to twist in the air and wrap themselves round the branches of the trees, to twist the leaves, to float up into the clouds to shiver across the moonlit grass. It was a music of sadness born of our sorrow yet also joy, for how we had each other, were Gypsies and had somehow survived.

And I worried that the sound might be heard.

Four – Foxy

Whenever we found an injured animal or bird, we always did our best to help, Zuzzi more than I, admittedly. Often it was a cut or a broken wing, but sometimes far more serious. We never put anything we were helping into a cage so they were free to leave whenever they wished, but mostly they realised to remain with us until they could again feed themselves.

The first of our visitors to remain with us until the end of our forest sojourn was a feral or part feral black tomcat which found us in about March 1943. I saw the eyes first. Small yellow, peering at us from the edge of the undergrowth.

"What is it?" Zuzzi asked, then saw for herself.

Whatever it was, it could be no threat to us so we both watched it to see what it would do. After a few moments, a dark shape slowly emerged into the distant firelight and we could see it was indeed a cat.

Its steps were slow, plodding, deliberate and it did not put its front left leg on the ground. It came nearer, we saw it was injured; I wasn't sure if it was a true wildcat or a domestic one gone wild, but I suspected the latter. Zuzzi confirmed it. It stood for a few moments watching, and I could see something hanging from its side like a large leaf, then it took two more steps and collapsed. Now we could see that it was indeed a black cat, but with a huge injury to its side.

Zuzzi was on her feet immediately. "Wait," I said, "It could att ..."

She ignored me and crouched down by the injured creature and shushed it and touched its head. It made no attempt to claw her. "We must help it," she said.

"But we're not vets and we only have Uncle Vanta's medicines. What good would they be on a cat? I'll hit it with a stone and put the poor thing out of its misery."

"You will do no such thing. I thought you understood that with all the killing I saw – and you saw – we shall never kill anything again unless we have to. We must help it."

I sighed. "Tell me what you want, doctor."

At her orders, I fetched warm water and a rag soaked in horse radish. Gently she bathed the injury. Her hand felt its left leg.

'I don't think it's broken – I think it's come out of the joint.'

I couldn't tell if the cat was unconscious, but if not, it was compliant. She kept shushing and whispering, held the leg and suddenly pushed and twisted it. The cat gave a squeal and leaped but landed back on its right side. She continued bathing the wound then called for bandages – strips of cloth really – and put antiseptic horseradish ointment on the wound, put the flap of skin back and wrapped it in bandages. All this time, the cat made no attempt to attack, but it growled lightly sometimes. She shushed it until she was all finished, lifted it and placed it on a bit of blanket, wrapping it gently.

"Find me a hen's egg," she said, which was easy as by now we had encouraged some of the camp hens to live near us by feeding them bits of food. I knocked the top off and she allowed the cat to lick the yolk contents until its head sank down and it had clearly eaten all it could manage.

Over the next few days, she fed it on yolk and checked the wound and bathed it when she felt it was necessary, but gradually we could tell that the wound was largely beginning to knit. As he recovered, the animal became able to feed himself on any insect which he found – and there are a lot of different insects all year round in a forest. He also got quite fat because it was so easy to catch insects instead of more traditional prey. The leg seemed fine, too. Zuzzi had to cut off some of the loose fur and skin which was clearly not going to bind and when, eventually, the animal recovered and grew new skin, it always had a patch of hairless skin on its left side which was only partly covered by its other fur. Inevitably, we called him Patch.

I don't say we were getting blasé about the war, but we thought less and less of it because we were feeling so safe. Sometimes, we heard aircraft going over the forest in one or other direction, but we had no way of knowing whose aircraft they were. On rare occasion, we heard gunshots in the wood, but a long way away and we thought this must be hunters rather than soldiers. I suppose there was no reason why the Nazis would want to come into the wood in any case because there was nothing here for them. The nearest villages were several miles away and we kept away from them so that we could not be betrayed. I often worried that one day, lots of Nazis might arrive with the Herr Reichmarshall to hunt like the SS had said. Zuzzi was convinced that this claim was simply a ruse to put we Roma at our ease, just the ones about owning a piece of land in the wood, and being well fed and looked after' in the camps and the other things they said to her family.

Five – Zuzzi

One day, something quite extraordinary happened. It was a pleasant, warm, mid-spring day in 1943 and I heard a horse's neigh. For a few moments, I feared it was the Germans. Foxy was away finding bits and pieces of food in the forest to bring back as well as selected firewood. I did not dare leave our little compound but crawled through one of the several escape holes which we had made by then to look in the direction of where I had heard the horse. The horse kept whinnying and I could tell it was getting closer and closer. Eventually, I could just see it in the distance weaving in and out of trees. I expected to see it with someone mounted on its back, but when it finally emerged from the trees I saw it was riderless. It raised its head in the air and seemed to be sniffing. My heart probably stopped at that point, because I realized with a colossal shock that I was looking either at Bavalengro or at his double.

I crawled through the exit hole and began walking towards him, convinced that I was seeing a mirage or a ghost or that I was totally wrong and disillusioned. Suddenly, he seemed to get my scent and galloped towards me at full rate, and my walk became a run too, both of us only veering and stopping at the last moment. He pushed his head into my chest and whinnied repeatedly, gently, quietly, as if he was telling me how he had at last found me and I hugged and hugged his neck whilst he whimpered little noises of pleasure.

But Grandpa's words came back to me. He was not my horse. He could never be my horse because he had been promised total freedom and that was a condition of his allowing us to operate on him and save his life. But nothing could stop me throwing my arms round his neck and wetting his long nose with my tears, sobbing into his ears stroking his face and his neck, weeping as if I had found my long-lost brother.

"Oh, Bavalengro," I said. "How on earth have you found me?" Then I realised how selfish that sounded. "I mean, how have we managed to meet again? How can you possibly be here now, all these months since and hundreds of kilometres from where we were parted?" I stroked his side and felt his hair was rough and unkempt, but that he was well fed and in good condition. I had no suitable comb there or I would have groomed him immediately, but, instead, I hung my arms round his neck and held him and squeezed him and kissed him for what felt like eternity. Finally, he pushed my arms away and nudged me in the old way that he had done in the past. I just couldn't resist it. I put my hand on his neck and the other hand on his back, heaved myself up, and sat astride him. He gave a whinny of pleasure and agreement. Of course, there were no reins let alone the saddle, but as I have said before, we Romany people can ride any horse without a saddle and since he was such a friend, the last thing I needed was reins. "Oh Bavalanegro," I said. "I thought I would never see you again, my lovely brother. But I have not forgotten my grandpa's promise to you which I nearly broke. You were not mine, you can never be mine, and so that you are here is no more than a friendship of a free animal and a Roma lass who is hiding to ensure her own freedom." I jumped off and apologised. "Dear brother, I cannot feed you, I cannot look after you for if I did you might be seen and people might realize that someone here was in hiding. You know I am sure, that you are free to go any time anywhere anyhow, for that is how it should be."

Just then, Foxy returned. He was astonished to see any horse let alone the one that I had loved so much which had suddenly appeared at our little hiding camp. I could not possibly get him into Thorn Castle, as I had now begun to call it, but I walked him round to the entrance that we used and showed him where we went in and out. He obviously understood that he could not come through the tunnel but instead whinnied gently, quietly and then slowly wandered off to a patch of grass and started grazing as evening came on.

"What are we to do?" Foxy asked as we had our evening meal.

"We shall just leave him as he is," I said. "He's wild. No one will suspect that there are people near here and I rather think that if enemies came he would run away from them in any case. He cannot betray our hiding place."

Six – Foxy

Every day from then on for several days, when Zuzzi emerged from the tunnel he was somewhere nearby waiting for her in particular and always trotted over and nuzzled her and pushed her with his nose and she would hug him and kiss him as if they were again meeting for the first time in an age.

The feral black cat and Bavalengro were firm friends from the start, in fact we strongly suspected that it was Bavalengro in the first place who had somehow guided or advised Patch to seek us out, realising from very distant smells that his sister Zuzzi was somewhere. Being better at finding its way, perhaps Patch had acted as a guide for the horse, who knows. Patch also always stayed near and we would sometimes see him nonchalantly seated on Bavalengro's back whilst the horse grazed, as if on look-out duty. It reminded me of Uncle Vanta's fireside tales of animals which got up to amazing feats. Another reminder was the horse's sudden leaps and somersaults simply for the joy of being alive in a beautiful world.

It's a strange thing, but we Romany people believe that there are two types of horse. One is the normal everyday horse that you people have and which you use for work or to ride. We Romany people – both Roma and Sinti and the other groups, too – have a different sort of horse because it is one which understands our language. That is why when Grandpa Kekkanav first treated him, the horse understood his Romany and agreed to the treatment in exchange for freedom. Bavalengro was undoubtedly a Gypsy horse – the understanding of the Romany language proved that. Mind, I was never sure if being a Gypsy horse was because a Gypsy person had been reborn as a horse or whether it was the other way round, that we Roma were sort of reincarnations of Gypsy horses.

I felt we had got through the previous winter quite well, but we were suddenly faced with a new and unexpected problem which stretched our resources to the limit. She was the second of our adopted patients, a little girl. We were out one day near one of the main tracks through the forest, collecting food when we heard a vehicle coming. That was a very rare event, but we were well rehearsed and within seconds we were deep in the undergrowth where we could see but not be seen.

It stopped on the track about fifty metres away and we saw it was not a German army vehicle, as we had feared, but one of the common small trucks owned by richer peasants. A man got out of the cab – he was dressed in the way of ordinary Czech people in a flat workman's cap, an old jacket and old trousers. He dropped down the tailboard on the back of the lorry and took something out, which we couldn't see and put it gently at the side of the track. Then he returned to the truck and took out a second thing. He picked up handfuls of leaves and grass and seemed to be wiping the inside of the back of the truck and he threw the grass he'd used onto the ground at the opposite side of the truck.

When he must have been happy with the cleaning he had done, he fastened up the tailboard again, clambered back in the truck and turned it with I suppose a six-point turn and went off rocking along the way he had come.

As soon as we were sure he really had gone and the sound of the lorry had all-but disappeared, we went over to the spot to see what he had put there.

It looked like two heaps of dirty rags. It took me a few moments to realize but Zuzzi gasped and half screamed. "Children!"

She knelt beside one of them and now I saw that they were wearing the blue and white striped pyjama-like uniforms of a concentration camp like Zuzzi's had been. The front of one child was matted with blood and faeces; the other child also had bloodstains and faeces but not nearly so badly. I couldn't tell if they were boys or girls as all their hair had been shaved off.

The first child lay very still and was either asleep or unconscious; the other moved slightly and moaned. It is a horrible thing to say about people and especially children, but they stank.

"They've been in a concentration camp somewhere," said Zuzzi. "We can't leave them here. If they're being hunted they will have a terrible death if the Nazis find them."

She began to examine the one who was most soiled who I thought was asleep. She put her fingers on its neck, then lowered her head to the child's mouth. "This one is dead, cold dead," she said. "We can do nothing to help. Poor little devil. Who could do this to a child?"

Seven – Zuzzi

I saw then that masses of blood had seeped through the child's jacket and I presumed it had bled to death.

I turned my attention to the other child. "This one is still alive but very ill. It has an injury to the front also: we need to get it back to our camp so I can do whatever I can. I'll carry this child; you bring the other because we'll have to bury it."

"Are you sure it's dead?"

"Yes, it's beginning to stiffen with rigor mortis. It must have died on the lorry." Gently, I picked up the live child. Foxy picked up the other one. We made our way back, but as we reached a tiny woodland meadow clearing, I said, "We can bury this one here. It's a very beautiful spot. You can bring back a spade, hide the child for the moment and then when you bury it hide the grave well."

He laid the child with reverence in a patch of sunlight on the grass. At the entrance to Thorn Castle, he moved the branches at the beginning of the final path to our hideout and then the thorn branches from the tunnel entrance.

"I'll pass the child through to you," I said. He crawled through, turned to put his head back in the tunnel and reached out. At the far side, I gently handed the child towards him. The child gave a little moan of pain. I carried it to the entrance to our shelter, Foxy following me, and I lay a blanket on the ground. I was glad it wasn't raining as if I'd had to do her medical bit inside our shack, it would have been dark and difficult.

I unbuttoned what looked like a tiny blue-striped pyjama jacket. She had nothing on underneath and it was hard to move the jacket because it was stuck to her with blood. "We'll have to risk a fire," I said after a moment. "I'm going to need hot water."

"We can't," Foxy protested. "You know how far away smoke can be seen. It's too dangerous. I wish the child luck and recovery, but not at the cost of our lives."

"What do you want to do, then? Hit it with a stone like you wanted to do with Patch? I won't take no, we have to risk it. Use the driest kindling only, just so I can get some boiling water for making anything I need sterilized and for bathing the wounds. By the way, this child is a girl."

I meant to hurt him. A fire in the daytime frightened us both, but he did as I said. If you use very dry wood, you get almost no smoke at all, but the problem is always finding enough to keep a fire going to get the water hot and identifying which are the driest sticks – sometimes a stick looks dry as a bone but inside it's wet, then you get the smoke. He must have struck lucky, because there wasn't much smoke and before long we had a boiling kettle and a pot of hot water. I decanted some of the warm water from the pot into a bowl and used a clean rag to bathe the child's chest where the material was stuck. In her semi-conscious state, the child occasionally moaned. Slowly, I was able to peel the hateful material from a wound which gradually appeared from underneath. "Her chest has been sewn up with sutures," I said. "Someone who knew what they were doing."

I wiped away some more blood and goo. "I'll need plenty of antiseptic," I said, "and painkiller."

Willow is a very fine painkiller, usually made by boiling up the bark and letting the resultant concoction dry to a grey-white powder. Foxy had got a good deal from Uncle Vanta's store, but had in any case made some of our own so there was no shortage. Foxy made me a fruit drink with the sloe gin in it and some of the willow. It probably tasted foul, but I managed to get some down the child's throat – the child was obviously thirsty.

"What sort of antiseptic?" Foxy asked. There are lots – his Uncle Vanta used salt water, calendula, lavender, vinegar and iodine. But apparently, he also used to say that salt was not very good except in rare cases and salt on a bad wound was very painful.

Iodine also stings badly, but this time I said, "It has to be iodine, this is a most terrible wound beginning to go septic, someone has opened up all the front of the child and then sewn her back together again for some reason. I think that's what had also happened to the child that you are going to bury. How can anyone do this to children?"

Foxy said nothing but watched as I gently bathed the terrible wounds with iodine solution. I admit I did not think the child could possibly survive, especially after the awful state the other had been in. I dressed the wounds as best I could, then wrapped the child in a blanket and nursed it in my arms. I wanted to give the child milk but of course we had none. Then I remembered the goats. If they were still around, maybe we could get some milk from them.

Eight – Foxy

The little girl looked grey and pale of skin from lack of fresh vegetables and inhaling human crematorium fumes instead of God's fresh air. Zuzzi remembered how at Majdanek many of the inmates had looked a similar grey.

She sent me out of our hiding place through the usual tunnel and ordered me to find a goat or failing that a cow. I remembered that one of the farms near the lake had cows. I think I ran all the way to the hill above the lake next to the grave then skirted my way through the edge of the wood and down to the farm to a field where cattle were grazing. It was a huge risk, but I knew I had to take it. I had with me a little milk can which he had got from my family's main camping ground in the past. Milking a cow is easy enough if the cow cooperates, but usually they're tied up in a parlour and haven't got much option but to let you milk them. In a field, especially when you're trying to stay invisible, it isn't easy. I picked one of the white and brown speckled cows as they are one of the sorts supposed to be more co-operative than the others and though it kept moving to graze, I managed to squeeze and squirt nearly a full can of milk. I hastened back to the edge of the wood, skirted my way to the track by the grave then ran all the rest of the way, hoping no one had seen me.

In our hiding place, the little child was still either unconscious or asleep. Zuzzi told me to put some of the milk into a tiny cup and warm it slightly and then gently and slowly I poured bits into the child's mouth and it swallowed.

That night, Zuzzi stayed awake all night, sitting at the back of the tent and nursing the child as if it was our own. Early the following morning, before it was yet light, she sent me went back to the farm, but I was too late because the farmer was already up and about and just taking the cows into the parlour. I considered putting our case to the farmer and asking for help for a sick child, but dare not. Instead, I remained hiding, like the fox I was, until I saw the farmer put three churns out at the side of the parlour. When I was sure there was no sign of him, I took the lid off one of the churns and filled the can that way.

Every day from then on, I raided the milk churns to get a single container of milk – mostly cream as the churned milk had settled – and Zuzzi usually managed to get a good deal of it down the child. Zuzzi also got me to steal hay for bedding for her in the future and for Bavalengro. After a couple of days, she seemed to begin to emerge from her unconscious state. I wondered if it was a Gypsy child, but I spoke to it gently in Romany and it seemed not to understand. From the old prison uniform, which by now we had burned, we thought she might Jewish.

Slowly, as day passed day, the little girl began to recover. Most nights she woke up after obviously appalling nightmares, something she has never even now got on top of though she has fewer. She was very weak and could not yet walk and had to wear a kind of homemade nappy all the time which Zuzzi or I changed very regularly and washed thoroughly. Getting the sutures out was an awful ordeal for her. She trusted Zuzzi but was very frightened of pain and some is inevitable. We got a lot of painkiller down her before Zuzzi began; she started off by trying to prise them out with the tip of a sterilized knife. The sight of that brought screams of terror from the child. Then Zuzzi had a brainwave – she remembered the fork she'd brought out of Majdanek. I sterilized it and using scissors and the fork, Zuzzi was gradually able to get the stitches out. To celebrate the little girl's courage and fortitude, Zuzzi broke all rules and, with Bavalengro's permission, let her have a little lead-rein ride on his back.

We estimated that the girl was about six years old, certainly old enough to be able to talk, but she never said a word. I thought maybe she did not like to speak because we were speaking a language she did not know. We tried her with Slovak and with English and French, but she made no attempt to respond. We were convinced that her hearing was OK, so there was no reason we could think of why she would not speak. In the end, we decided it must be because her experience had been so terrible that shock had taken her voice. At first, we called her Shooki, which means silence, but sometimes when I was talking to Zuzzi, she misunderstood and thought I meant her, so we changed her name to Tickni, meaning Tiny.

Nine – Zuzzi

But I wasn't happy. "Foxy," I mused. "I'm not convinced that we should be calling her Tickni. If she's not Romany but Jewish, I don't think we have the right to give her a name which her own family would not have used. I'd like to call her Maria after my dear camp mother."

Foxy thought for a moment. "But Maria is really a Catholic name. If we think she is Jewish, surely it should be a Jewish name."

I nodded, seeing his point. Then I had a brainwave. "Martha!" I cried. 'That's a good Jewish name and it's close to Maria. Every time I say Martha I will also think of my lovely Maria."

"Okay," said Foxy, "Martha it is." And so she became and still is – well, apart from a few months when she was Maria. We've never discovered her real name, let alone who her family were, but it did not matter to us, she was a little child who had somehow escaped from hell. Often, we wondered how she had come to be there. I thought perhaps a poor mother in a camp had sold her bread ration to bribe someone to get her poor children away from their living hell and to give them to someone for safety, or maybe she had given herself to the pleasure of one of the brutal guards in exchange. Mostly, I liked to think that some kind person, full of love, had risked their own life to get two abused children out of Hades. Perhaps their intended destination proved unsuitable because if she and her sibling were going to other Jewish people, they were presumably already dead. Why the lorry driver just dropped them in the wood I can only guess, but I suppose he thought them dead.

We never discovered, either, why they were in the state they were, but now we know that in one camp there was a devil called Mengele who experimented on Jewish and Gypsy twins and even sewed them together at the chest to see if they could survive. That both children had huge chest wounds made me sick with suspicion. Poor little Martha obviously had something wrong with her internals after the medical tampering she had experienced because she had no bowel control and still has to wear sort of nappies even now as an eleven-year-old.

As Martha grew stronger, I took her for walks in the wood seeking wild currants, raspberries and strawberries as the season progressed. At first, she would not let go of my hand and in any case, she was not able to walk very far, but going out for walks seemed to make her happy. One thing was that she did not need to wear a nappy on those occasions. When we were out, we would look for useful things to take back to our little enclosure, sometimes nuts or berries or an occasional root of a special plant and I taught her as much as I could about everything around us. For instance, at one of the streams there grew a superb patch of watercress where we stuffed ourselves and gathered a big bundle to take back for later. Gradually she was able to walk further and when she got tired I simply carried her. We managed to get as far as the mound of the dead Roma and Foxy was always grateful to us for going that way to save him a trip because he wanted to be sure that nothing there was being touched. Nothing ever was, and the old vurmi were still there including the dark and white stones on the mound that is, until the day it did change. We were on our way to the top of the hill to overlook the lake, which Martha enjoyed because in the distance she could see animals which by then she had learned to love. We were turning back to home when I noticed something odd on the grave. On top of the smaller whitish stone lay an oval metal disc. It had a split from the longest end and was just held in the middle at that point by a small piece of metal. Printed on each half was a number and letters. I had no idea what it was, but it could only have been placed there deliberately. I looked at the old vurmi beside the track and saw now that a new vurmi had been added. It was a thin strip of battered brown leather about 6 cm long and half impaled on a twig next to the original vurmi. It could not have got there by accident. Most vurmi simply show direction of travel or the presence of Gypsies, but some can indicate special locations, like the stones which Foxy laid. I had no idea what a strip of leather meant or could represent. That it was leather made me think of horses and the Lovari. "Come," I half whispered to Martha. "We must tell Foxy about this as quickly as we can."

Foxy was as excited as we were. "It has to be other Gypsies," he said. "Who else would leave vurmi? And why put the metal object on one of the white stones which most Roma would know represented children? There must be other Roma somewhere in this wood. Will you go again as soon as possible and move the metal disc from its present stone to a different one to see what happens and also, perhaps, we could put a new vurmi of our own, three little hen feathers by the leather."

That is what we did, and from then on we kept a regular watch on those vurmi right through the rest of the spring. Nothing happened for several weeks until one day when Foxy was in that area and checking things, he discovered that the odd metal disc had been moved back onto the small white stone. It was proof indeed. And then he noticed something else. A very obvious new vurmi had been put beside the hen feathers and pointing into the undergrowth. It was a stick with one end sharpened to a point and no attempt made to disguise it. Whoever left vurmi there was confident that other Roma were somewhere near. I'd better let Foxy take up that story now.

Ten – Foxy

Yes, it was so obvious that it had to be another Gypsy, but I was still suspicious. Suppose it was a Gypsy who had been caught by the Germans and was playing for his or her life by betraying us. Then I thought that was a stupid idea, because he would not have revealed the vurmi to such enemies. Whatever else someone might do to preserve their own lives, there was no reason to reveal something which was really of no benefit at all to the Germans and couldn't have helped any prisoner either. Cautiously, I stepped into the bushes in the direction of the stick.

About three steps in, was another vurmi, bigger this time, a large stick with its end also pointed further into the undergrowth. I was much more confident now because if it had been some sort of trap, it would assuredly have caught me. And then, only a metre away from the end of the larger vurmi, I saw a wooden box.

Really, crate would be a better word. It was as grey as Martha's skin had been, rectangular, with vertical wooden slats and a wooden lid, on each short side with rope handles to carry it. Gingerly, I lifted the lid, half suspecting something awful like a bomb to explode. Well, I suppose it was a bombshell in a way because it gave me a great shock, though a pleasant one. In the box was a huge cheese, some eggs, bread wrapped in cabbage leaves and two cabbages. They could not have been there long or some rodent would certainly have gone for them. I considered picking up the box and taking it as it was, but couldn't help a stupid feeling that maybe if I did so, there was a spring bomb underneath. So, I just took out the eggs, which were in a large can, the cheese, the bread and the cabbages, replaced the lid and made my way gingerly back to our home. As I went, I whistled a little Gypsy tune in case anybody was nearby and could hear, but no one emerged.

As often as I could after that, I spent time in hiding near the grave and the vurmi, but I never saw anyone.

However, a few weeks later when Martha and Zuzzi were on one of their regular walks to check the graves and its vurmi, a second strip of leather had appeared near the first. Naturally, Zuzzi took this as a sign to us of another Gypsy. Gingerly, she entered the undergrowth following the stick vurmi and sure enough, there was the wooden crate as before. When she lifted the lid, it had a different range of goods this time – a large pack of real butter, a bag of tea and a tin of proper coffee which had a German label on and another good loaf wrapped in cabbage leaves.

She brought them home in triumph, but I was still totally confused as to who the Gypsy was who had left these things for us. Little strips of leather were just un-Gypsy-ish.

About a fortnight later, I was out doing my usual gleaning and Martha and Zuzzi had gone back to the grave. She'd better take up the story now.

Eleven – Zuzzi

I happened to look down towards the Lake and there saw a group of men carrying guns and rucksacks and beginning to make their way up the hill towards us. I grabbed up Martha and set off running down the track to get home. They must have seen me because they shouted after me and ran as well. I was utterly terrified and poor little Martha was screaming. I thought I would be able to escape from them until suddenly, two men stepped out from the undergrowth into the track in front of me.

"Stop!" one shouted, a small but heavily built man with a thick black beard and wearing a Cossack hat. I recognized badly spoken Slovak. "Wait," he ordered. "We you no harm. We not Germans. We look for you. We know young man with you, too, where he?"

I thought of all the terrible times I had seen and the murder of my own family. I thought of Majdanek and the suffering there of people and how when I escaped

I had vowed that I would not let the Nazis ever capture me again, but it was not quite as easy now. I had Martha holding my hand and huddled in terror against me, whom I loved as if she was my own child, let alone my own sister. I pulled out my knife which I had always intended to use to kill myself if the need arose yet I knew I would not have the chance to kill both Martha and myself. To kill myself would, I thought, leave that little girl in the hands of people who would torture her for any information she had, not knowing that she was now dumb. If I killed her first, which seemed more honourable, they would then catch me. Would I be able to withstand their torture? I held the knife in front of me and in my rather poor Slovak snarled, "One step nearer and one of you dies."

The man with the black beard roared out laughing, saying, "Little mother, you think we not shoot first before you chance of using knife?"

I tried to sound savage and determined. "Who are you? What do you want?"

"We said, we been looking you but no harm you. Please trust, we not German, we partisan."

I did not know what to do. I wished Foxy was there with me. "How do I know I can trust you?" I asked.

"We leave you food in forest near big grave."

"You?"

"Yes, us."

"Liar!" I exclaimed. "Whoever left that food left clues as to who they were, their race. It cannot have been you."

Now the bearded man laughed yet again. "Little Gypsy not be afraid. We Gypsy in band. He good man. He our doctor. He help us when we ill, he help local peasants who no doctors because Germans frighten. And you want keep secret, not play fiddle in night!"

I could hear voices behind. The people who I had seen coming up the hill were clustered on the track behind me. They did not look threatening. They were not holding their rifles aimed at me but just standing and watching. One of them I especially noticed, a huge tall black man in a tattered army uniform.

'Ne craignez rien, mon petit. Je suis aussi le français comme vous, Algérien. Faites-nous confiance, nous sommes vos amis,' he said. (Have no fear, my little one. I am also French like you, Algerian. Trust us, we are your friends.)

"Comment savez-vous que je suis français?" (How do you know I'm French?)

"Votre accent vous trahit." (Your accent gives you away.)

He could only be French and therefore genuine so I said, "Très bien, je n'ai aucune option mais vraiment à vous faire confiance. Par ici." (Very well, I have no option really but to trust you. This way.) That was

222

how I came to lead the partisans back to our own camp. Not surprisingly Foxy heard us coming and was on the alert long before we reached it. I gave him a very quick explanation. He was alarmed and worried but he trusted my judgement and quickly saw that these were not Nazis.

Jacob, who was Slovak, acted as their interpreter for everyone as we stood on the track near Thorn Castle.

He introduced everyone one by one, several of them – Jews Ludwig, David, Yuriy, Karim, Doc, Beata and Agata. The last two were young Slovak women: Jacob, Ludwig, and David were all Poles who had escaped from a camp. Karim, the black man, was an astonishing looking man, hugely tall and powerful, who'd been put into a concentration camp – not a prisoner of war one – for French soldiers who were considered sub-human, which meant anyone who wasn't white. How on earth he escaped from that camp I never discovered because with his size and his colour he must have stood out amongst everyone else. But the company was glad to have such a fearless man. As a devout Moslem, he had to pray at certain times, but it did not stop him from having a very active role in the little group of partisans. Because of his size, Karim could have looked quite frightening, but I took to him immediately because we were both French speakers. His home was Algeria and his ambition after the war was to help his country to gain independence from France because at that time it was still a French colony.

Their leader was the man with the black beard, a Russian Ukrainian, Yuriy, who had considerable military experience and was himself an escapee from a work camp. They stood together in a long line. They almost looked like a troupe of actors on stage except that when they bowed, they did so in a rather ragged and unrehearsed way. When we three laughed, they burst out laughing, too, and did little arm in arm jigs of delight that they had made us happy.

"One day," Yuriy said in his very broken Slovak, "I have stall in America sell hot dogs. I go there to land of opportunity where streets paved with gold. You all come see me, you free hot dogs many as wish till sick." He retched as if he was being sick, to Martha's delight.

Twelve – Foxy

The joy and laughter seemed to escape the old man at the far end of the troupe-like line up who I guessed must be the Gypsy in the group, because none of the others could be.

Suddenly, I gave a great gasp and lunged forward. I just couldn't believe my eyes. "Uncle Vanta!" I shouted. I ran full belt and threw my arms round him but the Vanta I loved so much and hugged now was not the Vanta of the past. His face had that awful greyness I had seen in both Zuzzi and Martha, but it was not even just that – it was the sallow greyish, waxed complexion of suffering and premature old age. Only one arm tucked round me to hug me back. The trousers he wore were some sort of military ones and probably for the first time in his life he wore boots. He wore a camouflage blouse and into it was hooked the other arm. On top, he had a heavy army greatcoat. On his head was a most peculiar hat. It reminded me of an Egyptian fez but it was made of dark brown leather and simultaneously I saw with a shock that I could not see any of his long black tousled hair. I looked him in the eyes.

"Oh, Uncle, I thought you were dead, but what has happened to you?"

In answer, he touched his lips with two fingers and seemed to throw them to one side as if he was vigorously smoking a cigarette. I did not understand.

"Come," said Yuriy. "We go our camp."

"He was badly injured by the Germans," Jacob explained as we ambled away from our enclosure, my arm still tucked round Vanta. Zuzzi had gone back for her violin but quickly caught us up and meanwhile Martha held Vanta's hand. "I found him in the undergrowth when I was out hunting," Jozef said. "I'd heard lots of shouting going on which I guessed was the Germans so I'd hidden myself. I suddenly heard someone running as fast as they could through the forest. He was being pursued by soldiers. They went out of view and there were two shots."

I gazed into Uncle's face and saw tears gathering in the corners of his eyes. This once great man with a heart of gold and the compassion of a saint was now only a part person, shrivelled, cadaverous.

"He had a huge head wound and his right-hand arm had been shattered by a bullet just above the wrist," Jacob continued. "He was pouring blood when

I found him and I thought he was dead. When I saw he moved, I knew he wasn't actually dead and had to do something to try to save him. I'm no doctor, but when the Germans had gone thinking he had been killed and it was silent again, I picked him up and draped him over my shoulder. His blood trickled down my back. I knew he could bleed to death so I made a sort of tourniquet for his arm. I took him to a cottage near the far end of the wood and the people there helped me lay him down and get him as comfortable as we could. He drifted in and out of consciousness. They knew of a trustworthy doctor who came and did what he could. He had to cut off Vanta's hand and wrist. There's only a stump there now. Worse, part of his skull had been nicked off and it's damaged his brain. He has to wear that leather cap to protect the dressings on the wound."

I wanted to stroke his head lovingly, but as soon as I touched it, he flinched. "It's an open wound," Jacob explained. "The best the doctor could do. Vanta knows his time is short. Worse, he can't speak any longer and he has forgotten a lot of things. As he slowly began to get better, we discovered that he was quite a doctor himself and when we started our little partisan group, more to protect our people than for other reasons, he was the obvious choice for our group doctor. *That*, he can still remember."

"I come later," said Yuriy. "I soldier Red Army. I show how kill Germans. Kweek!" and he drew a finger across his throat. Then both Zuzzi and I flinched. "Good kill Germans," he said, smiling. "We raid German convoys, lorries steal. Good Slovak people give us supplies. Bad Slovak people give us supplies but not willing. Some supplies we give poor refugees eat. War drive many people from homes." He gave a low deep chuckle. "We got name, we called PLZN, it Slovak, it mean Revenge of the Sub Humans Peoples."

We had reached part of the forest where there were few trees and several clearings. "Now time for sub-humans eat. You join, eat," said Yuriy.

Their camp was about two kilometres away from our own clearing in quite an otherwise dense part of the forest filled with pine trees. They had pitched four tents which were obviously ex-army camouflage ones, presumably stolen from the Germans, I thought. Here we met two other members of the group, Michael and Artur, native Slovaks and local people.

Apparently, they took it in turns to do camp duties and today it was their turn. They had got a good fire going and the smell of the burning pine made me feel I was bathing in an exotic fragrance, reminding me of the days we burned pine in our old camps. They were cooking what looked to me like a young boar on a spit. I looked at Zuzzi and she at me. There was no way we were going to eat any of that meat. I tucked my arm round Vanta and led him gently to the fire, thanking Yuriy for his hospitality as I did so. Vanta sat down wearily, but something about his inner love and compassion must have flowed from him because the moment he was on the ground, Martha snuggled up to him and from then on, she loved Vanta as if he was her own grandpa – two speechless people who communicated through deep love.

Thirteen – Zuzzi

We refused the meat that was cooking, but we did accept some very good bread, butter and cheese and a bowl of vegetables from a pot. It was washed down with tin mugs of some sort of red wine which could only have been ex German.

"Come," said Yuriy. "You come us. You be fighters. You kill Germans with us."

I looked at Foxy and was pleased to see he shook his head. "Look," I said. "What the Nazis did to our families was terrible and unforgivable, but we are not killers. If we can help your group we will, but not by killing people. I know you will say that the only way your country can be free of Germans is for them to be defeated and sent back to their own homes. We know this, and we know that some people will have to fight and have to die, but we do not want any part of that. What we do want is for the guilty to stand in a court and have to account for their crimes so the world will know and it can never happen again."

Yuriy scowled.

"This is getting very sombre," Jacob intervened. "They tell me that you Gypsies can play the fiddle better than any other people in the world, but you have never played it for us. We did hear distant fiddle music once in the wood and Vanta was sure it was Roma. So now is your chance."

I picked up the fiddle and bow, drew a long chord and began. I played only three tunes before everyone was singing along, dancing, clapping and Martha spinning like a top. Vanta nodded his head to the music. Foxy said, "Zuzzi, let Vanta have a go on the violin. He may be able to play still." He seemed to be enjoying the music. I pushed the violin under his chin and brought his damaged arm up to it as a prop for it. I placed the bow in his good hand, but not a sound, not a note, nothing came. He looked at the fiddle and bow as if they were strange things which he had never seen before and seemed puzzled what to do with them.

Then I began to cry. I saw that there were tears in Vanta's eyes and also in Foxy's. Martha came to the rescue – somehow understanding, she took the fiddle, put it under her own chin and drew a chord of her own across the strings. We had been teaching her to play it, but she had a long way still to go. Nevertheless, she played a little tune we had taught her and then almost everyone round that fire had tears in their eyes. Here was a child, a victim, a horribly damaged human who officially did not have human status. She understood little Slovak and little Romany and even less of the Nazi world yet young people like her and us were the hope, we were – we are – the world of the future and it would be in our hands as to what sort of world it would be. Above all, it had to be, both Foxy and I felt, a world of justice for all, where massacres could not take place, where the innocent could not suffer, where good ruled. A world where your skin colour or your race was unimportant but being a child was. And being a Gypsy didn't mean people condemned you. A world where religion, ideals, politics, only mattered if they were for the good of all people. A world where people did not have to be afraid to hide their identity for any reason. A world where good people like Vanta were valued.

Now Jacob explained about the vurmi and the food. "Even though Vanta couldn't speak, he managed to explain about the massacre but thought you might have escaped, Foxy. When we found the grave with the vurmi on, Vanta got very excited and was convinced it was left by you. We had no spare food that time, but next time we were nearby we left the food to be found with vurmi which Vanta left, but I don't know why he left the leather strips. He tried to tell us but we couldn't get it."

Vanta became very agitated, obviously wanting to explain something. His handless arm came from his coat and tucked itself round Martha so both arms were in front of him, the good hand as a semi fist as if holding something and jogged up and down. Zuzzi got it immediately.

"A horse, he's describing riding a horse!" she said.

Vanta nodded vehemently and pointed at Zuzzi.

"My horse?"

He almost nodded his head off. "You mean, you knew I was a horse person? You saw Bavalengro?"

His excitement knew no bounds. "Of course," she said. "I get it now, the strips of leather were to represent horse, to show he knew a Gypsy horse was there? That the Gypsies there had something to do with horses?"

Vanta could not contain himself, and as he bounced up and down in agreement, little sounds of pleasure came from his throat, so that little Martha nearly fell off him.

We returned to the music, Vanta obviously happier now he had managed to communicate. He tried again with Zuzzi's fiddle and bow, but still couldn't get a proper note from it. I asked Vanta what herb or plant I could use to help Martha with her bowel problem. I knew about 20 or 30, but with her being so young I was anxious not to use something which could make things worse. In answer, he fished a bit of carrot from a mixed-vegetable pan and held it out to me.

"Carrot?" I asked. He nodded vigorously. I knew it was one on the list and certainly it seemed to help her a little when we gave her carrots to eat from then on.

Perhaps, Lieutenant, Sir, you could find doctors who could help her and maybe operate and undo the wrong surgery the Nazis gave her.

Well, to return to what happened, the evening drew on, the fire started to die down and we decided we must make for home. Martha was tucked inside Vanta's greatcoat, fast asleep and Zuzzi gently picked her out of it, wrapped her in her own jacket and with many goodbyes and cheerios we set off back to our own enclosure, with a last special farewell wave to dear Vanta.

"Come with us, dear Uncle," I invited. "Come home." If he understood, he made no sign but sat stolidly.

The following morning, we were a little later than usual getting up and after breakfast, this time greatly improved by the gift of bread and butter, I walked the two miles to where the partisans camped. There was no sign at all of them, only the still warm ashes of the fire and the small holes in the ground where the tent pegs had been showed that anyone at all had been present.

Fourteen – Foxy

A couple of weeks later, they were back and we resumed our campfire sing-song the same evening. Yet again, the German wine flowed with many a wink and nudge from Yuriy as to how they had got it.

It was on this occasion that they told us how they had been operating far away to the west, but that in the early summer, some Czech agents trained by the British had killed somebody called Heydrich. He was in charge of the whole of the country on behalf of the Germans and was infamous as a very cruel man. He was responsible for the deaths of many Czech people as reprisals for the most minor infractions of the rules which the Nazis imposed. Worse, he was one of those who had organised the mass murder of Gypsies and Jews. But the effect of the attack on him, whatever its benefits, had cost a huge price. The Germans had thought that the partisans involved were connected with a village called Lidice and they had killed all the men and sent the women and children to concentration camps and erased the entire village in revenge. Thousands more people were arrested and killed or jailed even though totally innocent.

It also meant that the Nazis were keen to find any more partisans so they had become very active against all partisan groups. Several small ones had been wiped out and those supported by the British and the Russians had lost many people and had to go into hiding. Those groups had been getting parachute drops of food and ammunition and occasional explosives expert to blow up railways and bridges. Yuriy's group knew its days were numbered if they remained where they were, so they moved east and kept a low profile. It was during that time that they started leaving food for us near the vurmi to help us out, though at that stage they did not know we had a third human mouth to feed. The disc which they had left on the small stone was a signal. It meant nothing to me but in fact it was a German SS soldier's identity disc. He had been injured and taken prisoner by the partisans. Vanta had tried to save his life but Yuriy was adamant, "No save, he SS man. He die." Then he had drawn his revolver and shot the soldier through the head. The disc was a signal to us, apparently, that one of the murderers of my family had been killed because he had been recognised by Vanta as one of the men who had first arrived at his own camp. But oh, wasn't that typical of Uncle Vanta and his huge compassion that, despite knowing that the man was involved in the killings, he still tried to save his life.

This time, the PLZN stayed with us two or three days. They said they would come back and sure enough, about a month later they did. There were no new members of their group, but, equally, they had not lost anyone and they seemed to have been pretty inactive in the interim. Or so we thought.

They had announced their presence that afternoon by the simple expedient of standing on the track fairly near our Thorn Castle and shouting, "Hey, we're back, come and join us. We have things for you."

Of course, we were pleased to see them. Yuriy seemed especially excited. "We bring you special present," he said, back at their camp. They had got their fire going and most of them were sitting about the fire and chuckling and breaking into the latest supply of stolen German wine.

They had brought us masses of food including flour, yeast (which we had not seen at any point in the war until now), several tins of German jam and lots of tins of coffee. Real coffee, not the ersatz type.

Yuriy's joke was, "We ask Germans very polite, you please give us food supplies. Germans say, here, help yourselves, we take much. We leave Germans dead." And he burst out laughing. We looked at each other and both were thinking that attacking the Germans in that sort of way was bound to lead to reprisals. Worse was to come. "Now I give you special present," he said. "Look!" and he beckoned to Artur and Agata.

Those two reached behind a tree and dragged and pushed a German soldier into the little clearing. His hands were tied behind his back with wire. His German uniform was battered, mud stained and had spatters of blood on it. Around one sleeve was SS insignia. His skewed cap had the sinister SS Death's Skull badge on the front. His bruised face had dried blood on it and one of his eyes was almost closed.

"What on earth are you doing," Zuzzi shouted. "What have you done to him?"

"This man SS," said Yuriy. "He kill Jews, Gypsies. He Einsatzkommando, he special murder squad, they take Jews and Gypsies, women, children, shoot, very big graves. We bring him as gift. You playing with him. You make bastard suffer, big pain. Then you kill." He was like a cat playing with a mouse and slapped him a few times across the face.

I grabbed the soldier by his uniform lapels. "Why do you kill innocent people?" I hollered. The thought crossed my mind to kill him there and then, for Petal, for Roopi Silverfeet, Pretty Flower, Lazzy, Gran and the rest. Several of the group laughed at the sight of my anger, but their ribaldry made me see I was as bad as them and it calmed me down.

The German said something but we couldn't understand. Jacob translated for us. The German was trying to say that Gypsies and Jews were like rats and had to be destroyed. Otherwise, they spread crime and pollution and disease into the human race and this prevented people from being good human beings.

Again, I controlled my temper.

I made the man sit down near the fire next to me. "I want to tell you something," I said.

Fifteen – Zuzzi

I wasn't at all sure what Foxy was going to say or even do. I could see his anger bubbling and he was having difficulty controlling it.

"I want to tell you a story," he said. "One of the most important lessons of my life I learned at the feet of my uncle there. I'm going to tell you it – Jacob, will you translate? Look at me, German, and don't take your eyes off me."

"We were in the main camp one day whilst he was treating a Roma man who had injured his leg. I got into an argument with a Roma boy who was astonishingly black skinned. We were just getting to blows when my uncle appeared and prevented us, waved us over to the fire like I've done with you and crouched there and also waved over another Roma with a very Asian Chinese appearance.

"I will tell you a story," my uncle said to me. 'There were once three men, a Gypsy and two who were not Gypsies who had been working together in perfect harmony in the countryside and needed somewhere to sleep for the night. They went to a farm and asked if the farmer would let them stay there overnight and give them breakfast in the morning and they would pay handsomely for it. The farmer said he would be delighted but that he only had one spare room with two beds. His wife prepared the beds and then they discussed who would have the beds. The farmer explained that the third person could sleep in the barn in a loft above the animals where he would be perfectly comfortable. One of the non-Gypsy men volunteered to go to the barn and the Gypsy and the other man had a good wash and climbed into their beds. They had only just got in when the man from the barn came and knocked on the door. 'I'm sorry,' he said, 'but for religious and cultural reasons, because of one of the animals in that barn, I am not allowed to sleep anywhere near such animals which may contaminate me. I will have to sleep in the house.'

"Keep listening, Mr. Nazi and keep looking in my eyes. The other non-Gypsy said he would sleep in the barn, but exactly the same thing happened and a few moments later he returned to the house to say sorry, he could not sleep there because he, too, had religious and cultural objections to one of the animals which were there.

"The Gypsy said he had no problems at all with any animals and so he would be delighted to sleep in the barn loft. But hardly five minutes later, there was a knock on the bedroom door and when the two non-Gypsies opened it, there were the animals from the barn. One said, 'Sorry, allow us some dignity. We have religious and cultural reasons why we can't sleep in the same building as a Gypsy.'

"You know," my uncle then said to us. "It often seems like all hands are turned against us, but we should never go against our own people just because someone has darker skin or lighter skin or Chinese-like complex. We are all one family of God, it is not what religion is or what country we come from, we are all human beings who should be caring for others and for the world in which we live – remember that lesson," he said to me. And so, we Gypsies are not racist people, we can't be. We have been the victims of racism ever since our ancestors left India a thousand years ago, so how can we ever be racist about someone else? We are leaves in the wind, fluttering from one place to another, full of beauty, leaves of red, brown, ochre, purple, black, hardly settling, but something which people like you sweep up and destroy, Mr. Nazi SS. You, Mr. SS, are like those animals."

The German said something which Jacob translated: "He says, Reich Minister Goebbels says Gypsies are disgusting parasitic vermin, and he was right."

"You know, Mr. SS, how terrible is it to say that? I've also heard Nazis say we are a polluted group who are no longer human, like the Jews. The strange thing is that we have become what we are because we are a generous and kind people. We take in people who need help, not because they are Gypsies, but because they are people like us. My uncle has told me how we have let in the starving, adopted abandoned babies and helped all less fortunate than ourselves – including Jews and Germans, Africans, Arabs, American Native Indians. We treat them as our own family, their babies are our brothers and sisters, which is why their skin can be dark or light. It didn't have anything to do with religion either, as Gypsies throughout the world have many different religious beliefs. Each taught us something – the oneness of God, his sovereignty, that we must be faithful, compassionate and peaceful with our neighbours. So we try. Look at my hair, Mr. SS, it has ginger splashes at each side of my head so maybe somewhere in my past I had a ginger-haired forebear. Is that racial pollution or human-ness?"

The German spat into the fire. He said something under his breath which was obviously something insulting. I could not catch what it was, but it made Yuriy very cross indeed. He took out his revolver and handed it to Foxy. "Now you kill SS bastard," he said. "He only good for deaths."

Foxy pushed the gun away from himself. "No," he almost shouted. "I will not kill him. Evil though he may be I have no right to take the life of another human being. I hate what he stands for, but not the human. Someone should have told the Nazis that skin colour or physique did not matter. Instead, they swept us up like leaves and composted us or burned us in the camp ovens. And no one cared."

Now it was Yuriy's turn to swear under his breath. He pulled the man up by his collar and half dragged him into the forest. Moments later, we heard a single shot.

Everyone round the fire seemed to take it as a matter of course. The exceptions were Foxy and myself and Vanta. In fact, Vanta sank his head and groaned.

We went back to Thorn Castle soon after and that was the last time we ever saw the PLZN because later in the War we heard that the Germans had ambushed *them* and killed them all. Vanta must have been amongst them. This time the Germans really did get rid of that saintly man. We never plucked up courage to tell Martha he had died – she loved him so much we couldn't give her yet another heartbreak in her young life.

I must admit, they had frightened and worried me in any case because I was afraid that if they were involved in attacks on the Germans near us, it might bring Germans to our place and that they might then find us.

I was proved right, but first we had two miracles. We do believe in God and some Gypsy people are

Christians, some are Moslem, some are Hindu, some Buddhist, some Jewish, but whatever our religion we all believe in God. I do not know, perhaps God wanted us to survive because one day, we had the first of those miracles.

Sixteen – Foxy

Early autumn, soon before dark and the weather cool, I heard shuffling going on outside the perimeter of our enclosure. I crawled through one of the escape holes expecting to see a boar or possibly a noisy fox. It was neither, but a nanny goat with its udder bursting with milk to such an extent that it was dripping. I am convinced that being a Gypsy horse, Bavalengro brought it to us realizing that it was in distress and would give both it and us benefits. I don't know where its kid was, but it must have given birth fairly recently; perhaps its kid had died or been killed by foxes or wolves or even humans. They normally have a herd instinct so maybe it was the only survivor of the camp goats.

I approached it cautiously. Goats are funny animals which easily take offence at humans who don't know how to handle them, so I spoke gently and it let me stroke it. As I say, goats can be very tricky to handle. They object very strongly to humans tugging, hugging, holding or pulling them and can attack, but I was keen to milk it. I got a can from our camp, approached it again, shushed and stroked it. I leaned down to try to squirt milk, but it would not co-operate at all and walked away, grumbling as it did. I thought of swearing at it, but if a goat thinks you are being aggressive, it can turn on you.

Suddenly, it twisted its mouth and put its head back to scent something – in the wild it would be predators or fellow goats.

Out of his favourite patch of wood came Bavalengro, snorting and neighing softly. I thought he'd come to see us – oh no. He went straight to the nanny, puffing down his nostrils and whinnying softly, nudged it with his long nose and appeared to be talking to it in Goatee; he backed off a few steps and watched as I stroked the goat again and went back to attempted milking. Now, she was completely compliant and from then on was always so, allowing either of us to milk her whenever *she* thought there was a need, however inconvenient that was to us. Later, she and Martha took a shine to each other and the one person you could be sure she would co-operate with was Martha. We regularly fed the goat grain we had collected before and it obviously enjoyed that, especially when we threw in a few molasses which many grazing animals love (just ask for Bavalengro's opinion!). From then on, the goat made frequent visits to the edge of our enclosure, I would say always once a day and often it stayed grazing for a whole day, probably in the hope of getting some bonus food. We always obliged.

The second miracle was laughable. We were looking for Bavalengro, who was always within calling distance. He came tumbling out and perched on his back was a hen we'd never seen before with several more scuttling along behind him. It almost looked like a miniature jockey on his back or a scene from a folk tale and the hen seemed to have usurped Patch. So now we had lots more semi-wild hens. It's very easy to find hens' eggs if you understood the sort of places they liked to roost when they have eggs and we could not risk adopting them, let alone clipping their wings, but they were a boon to us and did make life a bit easier. Hens nest somewhere very safe from predators so, inevitably, the middle of thick thorn bushes were an attraction and that meant that the few hens which arrived which were laying tended to nest in the thorns round our enclosure or even in the enclosure itself. The hens were by now very wild and so there was never a guarantee that there would be eggs for us but quite often they obliged. The following early 1944, spring, they were joined by a cockerel and of course that encouraged egg laying even more.

One of the hens decided Zuzzi's shoulder was a good perch and tried to get there whenever it could, and no amount of shooing would dissuade it. The secret was to let it settle and get a good grip and then it only became a nuisance rather than a pest.

Seventeen – Zuzzi

I don't know if it was because of the activities of the partisans – I think it was because they came from the direction of where the partisans had their camp – but a few weeks later, as winter drew on, we became very aware that something was amiss in the forest. The first clue was that when Bavalegro greeted me one morning, he was particularly fussy and skittish as if trying to tell something and then he turned and galloped off deep into the forest in the opposite direction to that which he usually took.

About then we heard motor vehicles, but did not see them. Next thing, a small number of German soldiers came along the track. We watched in utter terror through our entrance hole. With them, they had an Alsatian dog which was obviously trained to sniff people out. From the way it sniffed, we could tell it had found the scent it sought – apparently us. It moved its head this way and that until it reached the

249

point where we always left our path to our Thorn Castle to cross the track to go into the woods and follow the vurmi to Foxy's old family camp. There must have been several scents there because the dog was very confused and not sure which way to go.

"Zuzzi," Foxy whispered, drawing the knife from his belt. "Go to the shelter and lie down flat for fear of flying bullets with Martha. Don't let her scream. I'll stay by the entrance and if they try to come through, I shall stab the first one – I have no option. Don't let yourselves be taken alive."

Fear so paralysing that the mind seems to dissolve and run out with the cold sweat of one's terror.

All the time that the dog sniffed, the three Germans who were with it and its handler were looking round, sub machine guns under their arms ready for quick use.

Suddenly, the Germans found themselves under attack from an entirely unexpected source. The hen, which had always linked itself with me, flew from out of nowhere, squawked like mad and appeared to be trying to land on one of the German soldiers' shoulders. He put an arm up to defend himself and started to flap at it to get rid of that pesky hen. The next moment we heard a low growl and out of the undergrowth which was in the direction we took to the old camp of Fox's family and out came the old dog which we had frequently seen in the derelict camp. It threw itself onto the Alsatian and began biting it. It was a large dog, though old, and the force of the impact knocked the Alsatian onto its side. Confusion reigned. Then, suddenly, the dog released its hold on the Alsatian, turned and fled into the woods from whence it had come.

The Germans shouted amongst themselves and set off running after it. As soon as they had gone chasing the dog, Foxy got a tin of pepper and sprinkled it at the entrance to the hidden passageway to our enclosure. I hoped that if the dog came back, it would confuse the scent and stop it coming our way. Whether that would have worked, I don't know, because dogs can get scents on breezes and smell things several miles away if the scent is strong enough so our smell, barely 30 or 40 metres from the track, would have been easy. On the other hand, if it had taken a good sniff of pepper, its scent organs might have been badly interrupted.

In the event, it ended well, at least for us. We heard an ominous and expected shot and a single yelp from the direction of the old camp and guessed that the old dog had given its life. When the four soldiers came back the way from the way they had been, they were flustered and scratched from the various twigs and thorns. They held a hurried conference, making no attempt to get the dog sniffing again, and set off in the direction from which they had come. We breathed a great sigh of relief. I'd been holding my hand over Martha's mouth so she didn't scream, but when I took my hand away, the little girl sobbed piteously.

We saw no more of those Germans, but that evening dared not light a fire in case they were somewhere near enough to see the glow, which was unlikely, or more worryingly smell the smoke. Next day, Foxy went gingerly off in the direction they had come from to see if there was any sign, but though he found tyre tracks there was no sign of the Germans.

That night, we did light a fire again, and as Foxy and I snuggled together in the shelter against Martha, the only sound was Martha's breathing and the gentle hush of the branches and the twigs in the trees. We held each other tightly and my eyes began closing. "We shall never be caught again, never, never, again," I whispered. "Promise each other."

Never be caught again, and Foxy's head felt heavy against my shoulder as a distant soft whinny from Bavalengro wished us a good rest.

Eighteen – Foxy

We managed very well throughout the autumn and winter of 1943 and had no more visitors, welcome or otherwise. The supplies that the partisans had left us and the natural food from the woods meant that during the winter of 1943 we fared fairly well, at least we did not go hungry. Spring came and a very wet one it proved to be, not that it bothered us because we had waterproofs which the partisans had gifted us. They were actually German capes so it was a bit like walking about with an upside-down funnel on your shoulders. But we were fine although I did worry that if the Nazis ever came and found those capes there, they would assume we had somehow killed Germans to get them and it would be a death sentence.

Zuzzi had no such fears because if the Germans had found us, she said they would either kill us there and then or send us off to a camp. The capes were irrelevant in her eyes.

Bavalengro did not like the rain and spent lots of time just standing under trees to get as much shelter as he could. Patch was nearly always somewhere near Thorn Castle or in our shelter but unless the rain was very heavy, the hens did not seem to be bothered about it.

During that spring of 1944, the usual mass of woodland flowers and the promise of fruits and nuts to come were delayed and fruit and nuts were not as plentiful in the following autumn. We laid up as large a store of nuts for the winter as we could It's a good job we did, because the unforgiving outside world was coming at us though we did not know it at the time.

In September 1944, the Slovak people rose in revolt against the Germans, sensing that the war was getting near to its end. The Germans took over the running of the country from their puppet, a Slovak Nazi priest. We did not know about this uprising because, of course, we had no radio or contact with anyone else, but it meant that some Czech people tried to hide in the woods so the Germans could not find and kill them. Consequently, German patrols, for the first time, began to be a common sight. Fortunately, the soldiers were very inept at walking quietly and were usually in loud discussions anyway, so we always had plenty of warning when they were anywhere near where we happened to be. None ever came along the track past Thorn Castle.

We were just beginning to congratulate ourselves that we were doing very well, when several small groups of obvious partisans began appearing round our area. This was very bad for us because we guessed it would bring the Nazis. As much as possible we stayed in Thorn Castle, in hiding, only emerging through one of the escape tunnels when it was dark so we saw very little of Bavalengro and even visits to the goat were often difficult. We were getting through the food and not replacing it, as we should ready for the actual winter. I did not think we should light a fire because I was convinced that even if nearby partisans did not see the flames, they would smell the smoke and seek us out with whatever risks that brought. We had to have more uncooked rather than cooked food which is not as nutritious because the body often can't get the nutrients from it as well. It was not that we had fear that the partisans would harm us, but we had seen how ruthless the group which Vanta had been in was and we thought they could be ruthless with us and that we would suffer, or be forced to join them, even though I don't think our lives would actually have been in danger except had a partisan who knew of us been captured by the Germans, under torture the obvious thing to tell them would have been about us.

We had to be especially careful with Martha because her nightmares were bad enough as it was and scaring her about the people who kept appearing near Thorn Castle would just have made things worse. Equally, we also had to get her to be as quiet as possible and not put herself into any danger. She was loving playing the violin, but there is no bird in the forest which sounds like a squawked violin so we had to stop her.

Nineteen – Zuzzi

One day, when Martha and I were out gleaning what we could, we went to the gravesite and saw partisans coming up the hill from the direction of the Lake. I considered running but then decided against it. We sat at the top of the hill looking down on the men as they climbed up as if we had not a care in the world. The one thing we were sure of was that we did not look at all like soldiers. In fact, the leader of the partisan group, or at any rate the first one to reach us, seemed quite friendly. Of course, we did not give him any information which could have led him to Thorn Castle. Instead, I asked, "Have you any food you can spare us, please, sir?"

He gave us a little and it was from them that we learned the fate of the PLZN and thus Uncle Vanta.

We chatted with the partisans for about 30 minutes. They told us about the progress of the war and that the Germans had suffered several major defeats and were gradually losing. They asked where we lived and I pointed vaguely in the opposite direction to Thorn Castle. They were on their way to meet other partisans for some sort of operation which they had planned, but, of course, they gave me no details.

We saw no more of them, but as autumn faded into winter, the food problem became greater. Because more partisans were in the Woods, they were collecting some of the food which we would have used. They also had meat, of course, which we did not want so they were better off. We had no calendar, but round about Christmas time, the snow began. As we said, snow was always difficult because of the risk of leaving tracks which others could see. Whilst it was still snowing, Foxy went out searching for anything he could, but all food supplies in our immediate area we had long since gathered anyway. He came back about midnight, tired, wet and cold and with little to show for it. He had even been to the old campsite in the hope of finding tins or other food that we had missed. There was none.

We tried to keep all this worry about food from Martha, but Foxy and I decided that we would have to start rationing ourselves, though not Martha of course, to try to eke out the food. Most days in January it snowed: we would hear the trees groaning and coughing in the cold and the snow was proving a huge problem for the animals, too. We had no feed wheat we could give to Bavalengro or the goat and so both animals scuffed at the ground to get to grass, probably very poor quality by that stage of the winter, as it would have been. Nor could we solve the problem of leaving footsteps, which went very deep into the snowdrifts and were very obvious despite our attempts to hide them by swishing the surface with Willow fronds. We were increasingly cold and hungry and knew that we would not be able to survive until food in the wood became available again.

Twenty – Foxy

In the wild, foxes feed on insects, carrion and (when they can catch them) small mammals and birds. It wasn't so easy for a human Foxy.

One bitter morning, after a very cold night, I decided that this Fox would have to bring out his most cunning streak. "I'm going to walk into Poprad," I told Zuzzi.

"You can't do that," she exclaimed. "You've no papers and the first German soldier or Slovak policeman who stops you will arrest you and that will be that."

"I have to do something," I replied. "I'll be very careful and keep in the shadows as only a Fox can. I'm going to call at houses and offer to clear snow in exchange for food."

"No, madness!" Zuzzi almost screamed.

"Yes, I know it is dangerous, but if we stay here as we are, we will starve anyway. I don't feel that I have anything to lose. If it works, we can eat. If not, you always have your knife."

Patch, curled up at the back of our primitive shelter and beginning to look waif-like through hunger, woke up from a dream of insect-filled meadows on a hot summer's day and scratched an ear, seemingly agreeing with me.

Zuzzi's response was a huge sigh, but nothing was going to stop me. I abandoned the German army overcape and put on a thick layer of the warmest clothing I had. I had on my biggest boots, picked up a shovel, and set off. Naturally, I hid my tracks as well as I could, moving as much as possible through the wood parallel with but away from the recognized tracks. When I got to the wide track near Vanta's old camp, I saw the snow was very disturbed. When I examined it, I saw human feet had left the track and gone into the wood opposite Vanta's camp, but, more interestingly, there were clear marks of a sledge. For fleeting seconds, I wondered if somehow it could be Vanta, but that was stupid. Where would he get a sledge? And anyway, we knew the Germans had now killed him. Because of all the feet marks, I did not worry too much now about my own but followed the track made by the sledge through the wood into the town of Poprad. The first house I went to, I knocked on the door.

An old lady answered.

"Excuse me, ma'am," I said. "May I clear snow from in front of your house in exchange for food?"

The old lady looked me up and down. "I think, if I were you, I'd try the house next door," and she pointed towards it.

She seemed such a genuine old lady that I didn't think it could be a trap. I knocked on that door and a middle-aged woman answered. "Excuse me, ma'am. May I clear snow from in front of your house in exchange for food?"

"Who sent you?" she asked.

"The lady next door suggested I try here," I said. "I have two sisters and we are starving with not a bit of food."

"Tuck that long black hair under your woollen hat, Gypsy," she said. "Are you trying to get yourself arrested?" She helped me stuff my hair under my woolly hat whilst I flustered and tried to deny my race. "I know someone who I think could help you," she said. "Come with me."

Something made me trust her. I followed her through the snowy streets into the main street of the town. She took me to a baker's shop and peered through the window. "There is no one in," she said, "now is a good time."

When we got in the shop, a small dumpy man appeared from a back room. "Oh," he said. "What is this then?"

"I think you could help this man," she said. "Look!" She pulled my woollen hat off my head and my black locks cascaded down.

"Ah," said the man, "I see what you mean. Tu Rom?" he asked. I was astonished to hear my own language.

"Are you?" I asked.

"Yes," he said. "Well, my mother was. Who are you?"

I briefly explained. I did not trust him entirely so I did not tell him about Thorn Castle, but I said that I had two sisters and that we were starving and needed help. Please would he help us?

"Thank you," he said to the woman. "Leave him with me. I am very grateful to you for doing this." He gave her a small loaf as her thank you, then ushered me into the back room. "Sit down, boy, you have run a terrible risk. They have rounded up every Jew and Gypsy that they could find and sent them off to the East. I was lucky, I don't look Roma and the Germans never realized, though I suppose some good people in the town did. They have kept my secret. I had an apprentice here who helped me in the bakery, but the Germans took him to serve in their army as a Slovak volunteer. Volunteer? He was forced to go. That has left me shorthanded. How do you fancy coming here to work in my bakery?"

"But I know nothing about baking," I said. "And anyway, there are my two sisters."

"They can come, too. How old are they?" I told him. "Well, the older girl can be a sort of housekeeper here. The younger girl may be able to help with bits and pieces. I suppose you are musicians as well?" I nodded. "There is no call for Gypsy musicians in this town these days and it's far too dangerous for you. I can probably find you bits of work as well for pay as musicians at local events, but no one must realise you are Gypsies so any idea of playing Gypsy tunes or playing other music in a Gypsy way is out of the question. You understand?" I nodded again. "Your lives and mine depend upon it. Now, are you prepared to come here?"

"But, sir," I began.

"Not sir, uncle," he said. "You and your sisters will be my nephew and nieces."

"But we have no papers."

"Ah, that is a problem, but I think we can get around it. This is what we shall do. Go back to wherever your home is now, and take some bread with you to help. Tomorrow, you need to be at a particular place in the wood at two o'clock in the afternoon. Can you do that?"

"Yes, Uncle," I said. "Where do you want me to be?"

"Some afternoons I take a pony sled into the forest to collect wood. Follow the tracks into the wood to where the sled tracks end. Be at that point tomorrow at two o'clock with your sisters. Bring only clothes, and your musical instruments: nothing else, no tools, nothing that could mark you out as a Gypsy. And only bring clothes that Slovak people would wear."

"Thank you, Uncle. Thank you so much I cannot tell you how much it means to me and will to my sisters. But there is a problem. One of my sisters cannot speak and has trouble with her insides so that she has to wear a nappy all the time."

"We will worry about that later. I'm sure we can help anyway. Here, take this bread and avoid Germans and police at all costs. If I can get you papers, you should be all right here. We will make up a story as to why you have appeared."

"Thank you," I said again. I took the loaf under my coat, picked up the shovel from outside the shop door, laid it over my shoulder and set off back for the wood.

Twenty-One – Zuzzi

Foxy had an uneventful journey back to the woods to Thorn Castle. I was so overjoyed to see him back and hugged and squeezed him, so excited was I at his news. We split the loaf into three and gorged ourselves on it well into the night.

Next morning was clear but bitterly cold. We wrapped up Martha in as many warm things as we could then trudged our way out of Thorn Castle to the usual track and bit by bit, from there, again keeping in the woods, as much as possible.

As a fox travels, so did we. We crept along natural hedges, through thickets, along ditches and when we came upon a track we took a detour round or, if we had to cross, disguised our tracks after.

We had no clock or watch, but we knew we were in plenty of time when we got to the place the sledge was due to meet us. I admit that both Foxy and I were a little afraid in case of a trap or that we had been betrayed to the Germans. But we need not have worried. In the distance, we could hear little bells coming towards us and soon there held into view an enormously fat little pony, driven by Jozef the Baker. He turned the pony and sledge round, which now explained all the scuffing Foxy had seen before, introduced himself as Jozef, bowed to both Martha and me, and we climbed aboard. We gave him our last tin of German coffee.

Somehow, I knew this was the final chapter in our lives of hiding, but I couldn't help worrying about Bavalengro, the goat and the hens. There was absolutely nothing we could do about them and in any case, Bavalengro was a free spirit to go or do as he wished and was under no obligation to stay anywhere near us. That did not stop us all worrying whether he especially would be all right, but then, I reasoned, he was a Gypsy so he would find a way.

We slid into town and went round the back of the baker's. Jozef and Foxy pushed the sledge into a shed and Jozef led the pony into a small stable where he fed it with more grain than we had seen in a very long time. I wished I could have got some to Bavalengro. "That's the advantage of being the baker," he said. "If the Germans want bread they have to let me get my fuel for the ovens and supply me with flour and yeast and sugar."

Jozef Pekar gave us a room upstairs in which were three beds and we happily shared. It was like moving from the slum into a palace. Not only did we have beds, sheets, blankets and eiderdowns, we also had access to water from a well and, of course, food. Jozef used to bake very early in the morning from about 4 a.m. and would close the shop round about 1:30 p.m. It wasn't the end of his working day, because he would then have to prepare the bread for the following day for it to rise before he could put it into the oven.

When he had done all his essential jobs that first day, we sat in his little living room and drank local wine and ate the inevitable bread, but with butter and jam for the first time in months and drank the good coffee. Glorious! We talked until well into the evening and we trusted him, because he was a Gypsy, to tell him our own stories. Nothing we said came as a surprise to him because he had heard of all the terrible things that were happening to Gypsies and Jews. On my knee, Martha slumped into a deep repose, one which seemed for the first time not to hold nightmares.

At first, Martha was very cautious of him, probably because we had always tried to impress upon her the need to stay safe from people who could be our enemies. It was part of the upbringing for a little girl then to have to live in virtual fear all the time.

Twenty-Two – Foxy

On the second day, after he had finished his work, Jozef had an announcement.

"Tomorrow," he said, "a priest is coming here. He is to be trusted. He is going to take photos of each of you and he has some friends who can make good quality identity documents which the Germans will not suspect. Now, we must get you ready for his visit. And so you see," he said, "I go from being the man who shapes dough to being the man who does shaped hair. Now, good sir, if you will kindly sit in the barber's chair, I will do you nicely." He indicated a wooden chair for me. With a huge flourish, he put a small sheet round my neck, produced a pair of scissors and a comb and began the hard job of unknotting my hair and cutting it off in huge lumps. After a while he said, "That will do for now." He held a mirror in front of me and I was shocked at how little hair he had left me. I was about to stand up when he said, "Wait, I am

269

not finished." Then he attacked my beard, first cutting it as short as he could and then deftly shaving off the stubble.

"Now you, madam, if you please," he said, throwing my cut hair into the fire as is our custom. The sheet went round Zuzzi and he began, but not taking as much off as he had from me so that she still had hair almost down to her shoulders. "I regret, Madom, perms are off the menu," he said. "Madom has beautiful natural ringlets, but I also regret I cannot give madom curls."

Finally, it was Martha's turn, but he did very little to her hair before he was satisfied. "You do not have a beard," he told her. She looked almost relieved.

"You see," he said. "We have to account for you having to look different on your photos than you do now. If your hair was exactly the same, the Germans would be suspicious when they checked your papers and might ask questions."

I swallowed hard. "When?" I asked.

"When. You have to take your documents and be registered at the local town hall with the police. That is the only way to be legal in this town when we are under occupation. The police are under the orders of the Gestapo since the uprising and there are Germans in the town, who we hardly ever saw before and the last thing we want is to alert them that something odd is going on."

I understood entirely.

"And now," he said, "I wish to show you a bit of Gypsy magic. We need to find out what your little sister Martha will do when she is grown up. Who knows? She may be a future politician, a professor, a farmer, a musician, or, who knows, a baker or a Nazi or a bearded lady in a circus."

I looked puzzled. "I have here a magic bread roll." He flourished it like a rabbit from a hat. "Now, young lady, we must put you to the test."

Martha's eyes widened. She gazed at the bread roll in wonderment and reached out a hand to take it.

"No, No," said Jozef. "This is a magic roll. You cannot touch it with your hand only with your hair. It will tell us what you will do when you are grown up, whether you will be a good or a bad person. It never fails." He motioned for her to stand at the far side of the room. On top of her head, he balanced the bread roll. "Now," he said. "We will first find out if you will be a good kind person or a wicked one. Keep your head erect and walk across the room to me – the roll must not fall off."

It didn't. "Ah, that is good, but we must double check and see if you will be a bad person." He balanced it again, but to one side. The moment she moved, it inevitably fell off. Foxy and I were laughing now, but Martha took it very seriously.

"But wait, are you going to join the Nazis? Just because you are not going to be a bad person, doesn't mean you will not be a Nazi. Maybe you are so wicked the bread roll will stay glued to your hair. You must goose-step across the room to see if the roll falls off."

Entering into the spirit of things, little Martha began goose-stepping across the room, but she had hardly taken two steps when the roll fell off, as we all knew it would.

"Ah," said Jozef. "That is a great relief. You will not be a Nazi. Now let us try something else." He pointed to the far end of the room and once again placed the roll on the very crown of her head. "Now we will see if you will be a great lady," he said. "You must walk like a proud lady with your nose in the air to the other side of the room to see if the roll tumbles." Martha made a series of little steps, leaving her upper body as rigid as she possibly could so that the roll had no option but to stay perched. We all cheered her and she was most obviously proud at Jozef's prediction. "My my," said Jozef. "A princess if ever I saw one."

Twenty-Three – Zuzzi

Though he had no children of his own, Jozef certainly had a way with Martha. She quickly learned to love him and that balancing bread roll game was extended to cover a mass of other occupations in which, if she did not like the sound of her future, inevitably she moved so that the roll fell off. She had us laughing uproariously many a time especially when Jozef tricked her into telling her an occupation which she thought was a good one but was actually an awful one. Of course, she knew now that it was a game and she entered into the spirit of it with great glee. Later, Jozef taught her to juggle bread rolls, a trick she can still do spectacularly. It hardly needs adding that such used bread rolls always became part of the Germans' bread order!

The day after her first bread roll test, there came a knock at the back door of the bakery at about 2 p.m. There stood a black clad priest whom Jozef introduced as a Father Stephen. In turn, we had to stand against a wall on which a white sheet had been hung to have our head and shoulders photos taken.

But before that could happen, Jozef took a handful of flour and rubbed a handful into each of our heads so that our hair looked a little lighter than it really was.

After the photographic session, Father Stephen said he hoped to have the papers in a few days, but in the meantime we must remain in hiding and never be seen outside or in the front of the shop. Foxy had wanted to help Jozef, but it was something we just could not do at that stage. Instead, I did my best to clean the house and do washing in the stone sink in the kitchen whilst Foxy groomed the fat pony and cleaned the stable.

Just over a week later, Jozef came through from the shop into the back with three identity cards. He dropped Foxy's on the floor and slightly scuffed it with his foot so it looked older. He crumpled a corner of mine in his hand but Martha's he left pretty much as it was except for spilling a single drop of wine on it. There we all were, looking out from our identity cards, like respectable citizens. On each one it said, 'Place of birth Prague.' There was a very official looking stamp on each one. Each gave an address in Prague, too, which Zuzzi and I had to learn.

"Now," said Jozef. "You are my nephew and nieces and you remember that faultlessly. You cannot be Foxy, you will have to be Ferdinand as it says on the card. Zuzzi, your full name is Zuzanna, but you can still be called Zuzzi for short. But your little sister cannot be Martha. On this document, she is Maria Pekar. I got the priest to make dates of birth that were easy for you all to remember because you will be asked that. You must learn the address that you are supposed to have come from, which is in Prague. You cannot get it wrong when they ask you. What worries me most is that if they call Martha, Maria, she will take no notice. You must get her to answer to the name Maria as fast as you can. Then we must get you to the town hall to see the police to be formally registered."

We told Maria – Martha – that we had given her a new name of Mariamartha, but Maria for short.

As soon as he had a moment from the shop, Jozef did his barber bit again and cut all our hair even more so that it would not look exactly the same as on the identity photos. My hair, he cut extremely short now but he just took a bit off Zuzzi's and tied Martha's back in a ponytail.

So it was that with a good degree of fear, we made our way the next morning to the town hall to report that we had just come to live in Poprad at the home of Mr Jozef Pekar at his main street bakery where I was apprenticed to him and the other two were to be registered as household servants.

Poprad's Town Hall is an impressive building with a stone front and pillars at either side of the steps leading to the main door. German soldier was on guard at it and for a few moments we felt our hearts sink into our boots. But I went up the steps as if I had every right in the world to be going there. The soldier didn't even give us a second glance. We entered into the grand hallway with its deep red carpet and approached a desk. "We have come to register as living here in Poprad," I said in the best Slovak accent I could manage.

"Where are you from?" asked the official.

"We are from Prague," I said, as if it was obvious.

"Ah," said the man. "That's why your accent is odd. I'll get someone." He phoned and moments later a bored-looking uniformed police officer appeared.

"Yes?" he said.

"We have come from Prague and we are now living in Poprad with my uncle," I said. "Mr Pekar, the baker in the main street."

"Ah," the policeman said. "Baker by name and baker by trade, eh? He provides us with our bread. Not Jews are you?"

"Do we *look* it?" I asked, trying to sound weary at a stupid question.

He took our documents and looked at each of us in turn and compared us with the photo on the document. He was quickly satisfied and stamped the cards with the official town stamp. He wrote our names – our pretend names – into a register and that was that. We had succeeded!

Only once were we ever asked for our papers. Towards the end of the war a harassed looking

German officer came in for bread for himself and when he saw Foxy demanded, "Papers." Foxy produced them, but the officer was clearly happy and just handed them back.

Jozef was our wonderful friend who introduced us to people in Poprad who were to be trusted and I earned us a little pocket money playing Czech non-Gypsy music with Maria-Martha dancing and collecting in a cap at functions in the town. Foxy and I taught Maria-Martha to read to herself. Through the priest, we met someone who could do sign language and that lady taught it to both us and Maria-Martha which made Maria-Martha much more self-assured.

In the weeks we remained there, our huge regret was that we never knew what happened to Bavalengro or to Patch or to the goat. Bavalengro, I especially missed. We used to look for him in the woods whenever we went that way for fuel but never saw him. He was a brown leaf in the wind who, we presumed, had blown somewhere else, maybe with Patch riding sentry on his back and perhaps made others happy. Martha loved to be reminded of Patch who would only tolerate very limited human touching. He would give one severe warning which quickly became action every time Martha tried to drape him over her arms. In sign language, she called him "Raspy Patch".

We also learned that Jozef himself had experienced trouble with partisans who had stolen a lot of his yeast and some flour. We never let on that we suspected some of that yeast and flour had made its way to us, though he would probably have preferred us to have it.

I think the main reason we never had a great problem with the papers was that they were such expert forgeries. Another was that we avoided trouble and avoided being outside. Sometimes, I took Martha out for a walk in the town, but we were never challenged because, I think, the sight of a woman with a child did not seem suspicious to the Germans or the Slovak police. Foxy used to accompany Jozef from time to time on his visits to the forest for fuel for his ovens. When the snow was bad, we used the sledge, but when the snow went we were able to use a small cart he had and fill it with wood.

So we drifted through the rest of the war, until the time came that panicked Germans began fleeing west. We heard rumours of big battles to the south in which the Germans were crushed.

One day in March 1945, when Martha and I were walking in the woods near the edge of town, a soldier suddenly stepped out from the undergrowth in front of us. Martha, understandably, clung to my skirts in fear. I did not recognize the uniform.

"Who are you? Where are you going?" he asked in bad Slovak.

We had worked out a story for just such an eventuality because for once, I had foolishly left our papers at the bakery, an offence for which you could get arrested. "We have orders to go to a work camp and we are on our way there. You mustn't delay us or the soldiers might get angry with us and with you," I answered with as much of an urgent conviction as I could muster through my fear.

"Which soldiers?"

"The Germans."

"What nonsense is this? What do they want you in a camp for? You're not prisoners of war and they have enough to do running away from us." strange feeling came over me. Had I heard right?

'No,' I lied, 'It's the Germans who gave us the orders to go."

"There aren't any Germans here now. There was a big battle and they have fled, we are kicking their arses back to Berlin."

"Who are you?"

"Rumanian Red Army, part of Soviet Red Army. Go back to your home."

I couldn't help crying at the relief. The perceptive soldier passed a piece of chocolate to each of us to cheer us up. "Go home, you're safe now," said the soldier.

A few days later we knew we were liberated properly, though as Gypsies we still had to be cautious about our identity as some of the Slovak people were more Nazi than the Nazis and had been involved in murders of us and Jews. Nevertheless, the whole town held a big party in the street and we all felt safe enough to go outside and enjoy ourselves for the first time in years, but we remained invisible Gypsies.

Well, that's it then. What happens now? – We just have to read it all through and then sign it right? And you've put it onto a tape recorder as well. Will you be playing that in court? Sorry? The girls the Germans murdered and the mass grave – yes, I can take you to both. No, I never buried the girls. Actually, I never went back there. I could not face it. I wanted them to lie under God's sky and hear the birds and the bees hear the songs of the stars and try to forget the wolves.

So, you still have no news if any of whether our families survived or even Zuzzi's beautiful Maria? We keep a little hope.

I suppose you will say we are free now but we're not because there's something else we want to say. All the time we were hidden, we hardly ever stopped being afraid, true, but worse we could not stop thinking about the terrible fates of our families. The silence after the death of a loved one is deafening. We have both said to each other that we feel sort of guilty because we survived and they didn't. We can never get on top of the grief and we still have nightmares. We hope in time it will feel better.

Who is this man who has just come into the room? Sir, I don't understand. Zuzzi, why are you screaming? Who is this man who has just come in? Bum Nose? My God, Bum Nose? It can't be. This man killed Zuzzi's brothers, he watched children starve, he sent Zuzzi's people and the Jews to their deaths. Give me a gun, someone, just give me a gun. This man is a murderer, Bum Nose who Zuzzi told you about – Zuzzi, don't scream, I will protect you. Why is he here? Take him away. If I had a gun now ..., but Lieutenant, sir, you're the war crimes investigators. This man is a war criminal. Why is he not locked up in a cage? Why are you doing this to us? Zuzzi saw him, witnessed. Working for the Americans now? Economic planning for the new Germany? I do not understand. But we weren't criminals; they killed us because we were Gypsies. No, it isn't different from the Jews. Evil creates evil.

Zuzzi, Zuzzi, what can we say, what can we do? We are only Gypsies. Come, we can witness no more. Granny wanted the wolves caged. I have failed her. We will not sign your statement – there is no justice for Gypsies.

Postscript

The Nazis intended to kill all the Gypsies and Jews of Europe for racial reasons. They probably managed the deaths of over one million of the Gypsies – most books massively underestimate the numbers who died – and many more Jews. They probably included all the Gypsies of Estonia, Lithuania, Luxemburg and the Netherlands; most of the Gypsies of Belgium, Bohemia and Moravia, Croatia, Germany, Hungary, Poland, German-controlled Russia and Ukraine; more than half the Gypsies of Austria, Latvia and other parts of the USSR; many of the Gypsies of Denmark, France, Greece, Italy, Macedonia, Rumania, Serbia, Bulgaria and Slovakia. It is not clear what proportion they managed to kill in Norway or Armenia.

Special Nazi murder squads, the Einsatzgruppen, existed, especially in Poland, Russia and the Balkans. In some of these murders, they used killing of Gypsies as dress rehearsals for the even greater massacres of

Jews. The locations of many of the Gypsy mass burials are not known because no witnesses survived. It is not clear to what extent Slovakia was one of those locations.

In preparation for the proposed invasion of Britain, they created lists of the names of Gypsies, Jews and others they meant to murder. These were in good company – one of the first names on the list was Winston Churchill, the British war leader. Fortunately, the invasion never came.

Though survivors of the even greater Jewish massacres received compensation for their suffering, very few Gypsies ever did and, largely, their killers remained unpunished. Mengele, who conducted horrible experiments on Jewish and Gypsy twins, was never found but was known to have died of old age in hiding in South America.

Further Reading

AUSCHWITZ-BIRKENAU: The Past and the Present, 2009. (Guide book).

BARNETT, Ruth. *Jews and Gypsies: Myths and Reality.* Amazon CreateSpace, 2013.

BEDFORD, Stephanie and RAWCLIFFE, Barbara. *Porraimos: The Devouring.* Northampton, Northamptonshire County Council, 1999.

BOYNE, John. *The Boy in the Striped Pyjamas.* Oxford, David Fickling Books, 2008.

DAWSON, Robert. *The Porraimos: Photos of the Gypsy Holocaust in World War 2.* Robert Dawson, Backwell, Derbyshire, 2013.

DAWSON, Robert. *Never Forget: A Photographic Supplement to the Romany Holocaust.* Robert Dawson, Backwell, Derbyshire, 2014.

FINGS, Karola; Hensi, Herbert; Sparing, Frank. *From Race Science to the Camps: The Gypsies During the Second World War, Vol 1*. Hatfield, Herts, University of Hertfordshire Press, 1997.

HANCOCK, Ian. *Danger! Educated Gypsy*. Hatfield, University of Hertfordshire Press, 2010.

HOLM, Ann. *I Am David*. Lewes, Gyldendal Methuen, 1963.

HOLOCAUST CONTROVERSIES WEBSITE. Available at: http://holocaustcontroversies.blogspot.co.uk/

KENRICK, Donald. *In the Shadow of the Swastika: The Gypsies During the Second World War, Vol 2*. Hatfield, Herts, University of Hertfordshire Press, 1999.

KENRICK, Donald and PUXON, Grattan. *The Destiny of Europe's Gypsies*. London, Chatton Heinemann for Sussex University Press, 1972.

KENT CC. *Gypsies and the Holocaust*. Kent County Council, c 1985.

KERR, Judith. *When Hitler Stole Pink Rabbit*. London, Puffin, 1971.

LAGNADO, Lucette Matalon, and DEKEL, Sheila Cohn. *Children of the Flames: Dr Jozef Mengele and the Untold Story of the Twins of Auschwitz*. London, Sidgwick and Jackson, 1991.

LOWRY, Lois. *Number the Stars*. Boston, Houghton Mifflin, 1989.

NYISZLI, Miklos. *I Was Doctor Mengele's Assistant*. Oswiecim, 2010.

ROY, Jennifer. *The Yellow Star.* Singapore, Marshall Cavendish, 2006.

SMITH, Lyn. *Forgotten Voices of the Holocaust.* London, Ebury Press, 2005.

WAGENAAR, Aad. Translated by Janna Eliot, Afterword by Ian Hancock. *Settela.* Nottingham, Five Leaves Publications, 2005.

ZUSAK, Markus. *The Book Thief.* New York, Knopf and Doubleday, 2006.